"I'm as qualified as

"No, you're not," Erin teased. "You've never been engaged, so I've come closer to actually getting married."

Cade got up and crossed the room to her. "That gives you a little experience, but I've got a lot because I spent fifteen years growing up as the child of a bad marriage," Cade said. "That makes my advice more valid."

"You were going to stay on your side of the room tonight."

"See—this is why I shouldn't get married. I didn't do what I said I would. Scared of me?"

"Not in the least. I have no intention of marrying you. Now you go back to your side of the room and think about my brother."

"I want to know something else. Give me a straight answer. Did you miss any sleep after our first kiss?"

"Cade, we aren't going to do this."

"I think you just answered my question," he said in a husky voice as his gaze lowered to her mouth.

She couldn't catch her breath.

* * *

The Rancher's Nanny Bargain is part of the Callahan's Clan series—A wealthy Texas family finds love under the Western skies!

Dear Reader,

One of the most binding ties of friendship is trust. Multimillionaire Texan Cade Callahan is caught between honoring the trust of his lifelong best friend or breaking that trust by yielding to the sizzling attraction of his best friend's younger sister, Erin Dorsey, who is also Cade's new nanny. At the same time, Erin is struggling to resist the appealing rancher, a confirmed bachelor, who is the kind of man she has always avoided. Erin does not want any emotional complications that will interfere with her career goals—but she can't resist Cade's kisses. Changing both Erin's and Cade's lives is the baby girl in their care.

This story features the second Callahan brother, an exciting, handsome, wealthy rancher who is a cowboy at heart. He hires a strong woman who knows what she wants and changes his life in ways he thought would be impossible.

Meet another Texas Callahan...

Sara Orwig

SARA ORWIG

THE RANCHER'S
NANNY BARGAIN

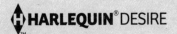

HARLEQUIN® DESIRE

Recycling programs
for this product may
not exist in your area.

ISBN-13: 978-0-373-83820-2

The Rancher's Nanny Bargain

Printed in U.S.A.

www.Harlequin.com

Sara Orwig is an Oklahoman whose life revolves around family, flowers, dogs and books. Books are like her children: she usually knows where they are, they delight her and she doesn't want to be without them. With a masters degree in English, Sara has written mainstream fiction, historical and contemporary romance. She has one hundred published novels translated in over twenty-six languages. You can visit her website at www.saraorwig.com.

Books by Sara Orwig

Harlequin Desire

Lone Star Legends

The Texan's Forbidden Fiancée
A Texan in Her Bed
At the Rancher's Request
Kissed by a Rancher
The Rancher's Secret Son
That Night with the Rich Rancher

Callahan's Clan

Expecting the Rancher's Child
The Rancher's Baby Bargain

Visit her Author Profile page at Harlequin.com, or saraorwig.com, for more titles.

To Stacy Boyd with so many thanks
for being my editor. To Maureen Walters
with special thanks for all the years together.
With love to David and to our family.

One

In his office at his ranch house, Cade Callahan sorted mail that had come while he was in Dallas at his commercial real estate office the past two days. But the letters blurred before his eyes.

All he could think about was the loss of his younger brother and his sister-in-law in the last week of June. How many times would he replay in his mind the moment he imagined their car had been struck by a drunk driver? Nate had been killed instantly, and Lydia had died on the way to the hospital. The drunk driver who hit them had died at the scene.

And Cade had been left as the sole guardian of his six-month-old niece, Amelia.

A shiver went down his spine as it always did when he thought about the tremendous responsibility he'd inherited. He knew nothing about caring for a baby. Which was why he needed Erin Dorsey.

He glanced at his watch. Within minutes she would arrive for an interview for the nanny job. He had high hopes for her.

At lunch, more than a week ago, with his closest friend, Luke Dorsey, Cade had complained about being unable to find a suitable nanny despite all the interviews he'd had. Luke had a surprising recommendation—his sister.

Recalling Luke's younger sister Erin, Cade had remembered a timid, freckle-faced, scrawny little redhead, hovering in the background and keeping away from Luke and his friends. Cade hadn't ever said more than hello to her and barely had received more than that in return before she'd disappeared from sight. She was years younger, probably twenty or twenty-one now.

When he'd mentioned to Luke that she was very quiet and very young, Luke's blue eyes had twinkled.

"Not as quiet as when she was a kid," he'd said. "And young is good. She's energetic, upbeat, loves kids and they love her. Trust me, she's great taking care of kids."

"Is she an environmental engineer like you?"

"Not at all." He'd gone on to list her credentials: an undergraduate degree in Human Development and Family Services, director of her church nursery, member of the Big Sister program while in college. "The only drawbacks for her would be a time limit and living on your ranch."

"What's the time limit?" Cade had asked, even though he'd had no intention of hiring Luke's little sister.

"Erin just finished her bachelor's degree. She'll be starting back at the University of Texas for her master's in January. She's staying out a semester to earn money. I've offered to pay for school but she won't accept my offer." He'd grinned. "My sister is independent and wants to do it her way. Frankly, I can understand. We're a big family and it will help Mom and Dad. I put myself through, something you know nothing about as Dirkson Callahan's son who set all of you up in business."

"Not Blake. Don't get me started on my dad, or my mom. Mom won't keep Amelia at all and made that plain from the first and flew to Europe with friends. Why the hell my dad had so many kids... Anyway, this is August, so it won't help me to hire a nanny for a few months and then start over," Cade had said before biting into a thick, juicy rib covered in dark red barbecue sauce.

"Think about it before you say no," Luke had replied. "Hiring Erin now would give you time to get a really good nanny, and before she has to leave she could help you select the perfect replacement and train her. It would remove the pressure that you're under now to choose a nanny quickly no matter how little you like any of them."

He'd felt a slight bit defensive. "They all come highly recommended. I hate turning a baby over to a stranger, but I have to do something quickly.

Grandmother and my cook have been taking care of Amelia and Grandmother doesn't know much more about babies than I do. Maisie cooks, so she can't care for Amelia all of the time. Sierra, Blake's wife, has helped, too."

"Hire Erin and you won't be turning your niece over to a stranger."

Maybe not a complete stranger, but he barely knew Erin and he hadn't even seen her since he'd graduated from high school. He knew Luke's argument to that—Cade had known his family since they were both kids. He knew he could trust her and believe what Luke told him about her.

"I wouldn't recommend my sister to some of my friends," Luke had said, "but I know I can leave the country and be certain you won't hit on her."

Amen to that one, Cade had thought, but he hadn't say it aloud. "Well, hell—"

"You won't hit on her because she's not your type. She takes life seriously, while I know you're a care-free, love-'em-and-leave-'em guy. Last year when the guy she was engaged to broke their engagement to marry someone else, she was crushed and she hasn't gotten back into dating since then."

Cade had been surprised to hear she had been engaged, but he'd said nothing. He still could only think of her as a waif who drifted in the background of Luke's life. In addition to Erin, there were four younger kids in Luke's family and they, too, had usually avoided Luke's crowd.

"She has told a few people, but should you call her,

I think you ought to know... While she was engaged, she was pregnant with his baby. She miscarried and that's why the guy broke off the engagement. The doctors said she might be able to have a baby, but there was a higher than normal chance she might miscarry again. Her ex-fiancé said he wanted to know for certain that he had married a wife who could give him kids."

"Well, damn, he must not have been deeply in love."

"That's what I thought, but what do I know—or you for that matter—about love and marriage? The breakup left her shaken and brokenhearted. We have a big family and she loves babies, so that loss tore her up because she wants marriage and kids. Plus she was in love with her fiancé. Now she doesn't trust her own judgment in men. In short, she's vulnerable. I know I can trust you not to cause her more grief."

"If she works for me, some of the guys who work for me might ask her out, but she should be able to deal with them."

"She'll handle them, I'm sure. And I won't have to worry about you, especially since you know this about her."

"You act as if I've agreed to call her."

"Go interview some more nannies and then you'll call Erin."

"It's a shame you don't have any confidence in yourself," Cade had remarked.

Luke had laughed, then quickly sobered. "Look, Cade, she's had a rough year and I'd like to see her where she can focus on a baby and get back to normal living. Take my advice. Stop worrying and get someone you know who can do the job."

"I'll think about it. Tell me again, what is it you're doing?"

Luke smiled. "I'm an environmental engineer and I'll be working for the government in Antarctica on wastewater management, permitting, removal of solid and hazardous waste—mainly effective wastewater treatment in the Antarctic which is not the same as in Texas—"

"I've got it. At least I've got as much as I want to hear about what you do. I'll think about your sister," he repeated.

Two days of interviews later, Cade contacted her.

Unable to get the image of a solemn, skinny kid out of his thoughts, he expected the same whispered, minimal conversation he'd got from her when they were kids, but was surprised to find the grown-up Erin friendly and confident. She'd turned him down politely, thanking him for the offer, preferring to keep her high-paying secretarial job until she went back to school.

But Cade had taken Luke's advice to heart. He knew exactly what he needed: someone he knew, someone he could trust to watch baby Amelia. Using all his powers of persuasion, he'd convinced Erin to come interview before she made a hasty decision.

Now in his office at the ranch he glanced at the clock and saw she was due in four minutes.

As he shifted his attention to the papers in front of him, there was a light rap on the door. His tall, blond butler stood waiting. "Miss Dorsey has arrived."

He smiled to himself. Erin Dorsey was as punctual as Mary Poppins. "Thanks, Harold. Tell her to come in."

Harold stepped out of sight and in seconds she walked into the room.

For an instant Cade forgot his nanny interview. He could only stare at the tall, leggy redhead who entered the room. Blond streaks highlighted her long red hair that fell in curls around her face, framing her long-lashed green eyes. She wore what should have been a tailored, ordinary businesslike navy suit with a V-neck white blouse. On her, though, it was anything but ordinary or businesslike. The short skirt revealed long, shapely legs while a narrow belt circled a tiny waist. In a million years he would never have recognized her as Luke's younger sister.

Dazed, he stared at her until he realized what he was doing. Then he stood and closed the distance between them as she offered her hand. When his fingers wrapped around her soft hand, the contact startled him again.

"You've grown up since I last saw you," he said, causing her to smile, revealing a dimple in her right cheek. He didn't remember any dimple, but he also didn't remember seeing her smile as a little kid. But then again, he hadn't ever paid attention to her. Now, her dazzling, dimpled smile sent the temperature in the room climbing. For an instant he thought he couldn't hire her as a nanny because he wouldn't be able to resist flirting with her or wanting to kiss that delicious mouth. Somehow he managed to shake that thought and pull himself back to business in time to hear her speak.

"I believe you have, too. I'm not still Luke's ten-year-old kid sister which was probably the last time we saw each other."

He bit back the reply that she sure as hell wasn't. He waved his hand slightly toward two brown leather chairs that faced his wide cherrywood desk. "Please, have a seat," he said. When she sat, he turned the other chair to face her.

He had already decided before she arrived that he wanted her for the job because he knew her and could trust her. More importantly, he knew her family values and they were what he viewed as ideal, what he wanted for his baby niece. Luke's family was the family he always wished he'd had—caring and supportive of each other. His parents were invested in their kids and Luke had had his dad's guidance and friendship—things that Cade had never known from his dad beyond financial support. Yes, Erin would be the perfect nanny in so many important ways. He would just have to resist her stunning looks and assume his normal professional manner.

"It's been a long time since I last saw you," he said, smiling at her.

She flashed a warm smile in return. "I'm surprised you remember me at all. I tried to stay out of Luke's way when he had high school friends over. In those days tall, noisy boys intimidated me."

Looking at her now, he doubted if any male intimidated her, because Luke's sister had become a gorgeous, poised woman. Just the kind of woman that he hoped Amelia would one day grow up to be. As he thought about his little niece, he felt the too familiar dull ache that came each time he thought about her parents. He missed his brother and he always would. Little Amelia should have Nate and Lydia instead of an uncle and a nanny.

As if Erin guessed his thoughts, her smile vanished. "I'm so sorry about your brother and sister-in-law."

"It was a tragedy. The drunk driver who hit them died in the crash, too. Three lives lost," he replied, still thinking about his brother.

"At least their baby wasn't with them, and how wonderful for you to be her guardian."

"It's an awesome responsibility and one that I never expected to have," he replied, his thoughts shifting from Nate to Amelia. "You know, when Nate was working on their wills and he asked me if I would be Amelia's guardian, I thought the likelihood of this ever happening was zero." He remembered how shocked and dazed he had been over Nate's and Lydia's deaths back in June and how downright awestruck he'd been when he'd realized he had full responsibility for Amelia and would be his little niece's guardian. "I don't know one thing about babies."

"Luke said your niece is six months old now."

"That's right." He nodded. "Luke said you have experience taking care of babies and little kids. I—"

"Cade, I have to be honest with you." She didn't hesitate after her interruption. "As tempting as this job is, I have to decline. Out of courtesy to my brother, I'm here to talk to you, but I don't see changing from the secretarial job I have till school starts." Smiling, she shook her head. "I'm sorry, but this won't work out. We can both tell Luke we tried."

"Don't be too hasty. Let's talk about it," Cade said, unable to resist a glance as she crossed her long legs. How did that wisp of a shy, plain kid grow into this gorgeous, leggy redhead?

Once again he had to shift his thoughts to the reason for the interview.

"Before you turn down this job, listen to what I have to offer. My grandmother is currently minding Amelia, here on the ranch. Grandmother can't deal with the care of a baby on a permanent basis. In fact, she can't deal with it for many more days. Anyway, at least meet Amelia and then let's talk."

"That seems unnecessary because I can't take the nanny job."

"The nanny job will fit in a lot more with the degrees you're getting to work with children," he reminded her. "Also, your brother is going to ask us both about our interview and it'll make him a lot happier if you at least listened to my offer. Besides," Cade added, smiling at her, "how much time does it take to meet a baby?"

There was a flicker in the depths of her green eyes

and for another electric moment, he was tempted to forget about Luke and the nanny job and just enjoy the beautiful woman who sat in front of him.

Then she blinked, glanced away and the moment vanished, but it resonated long after. It was another warning that hiring her might not be as problem-free as he had hoped. But as long as she could take good care of Amelia, he could resist the volatile chemistry that had to be off-limits.

"I suppose you're right," she said, nodding. "All right, I'll meet Amelia and we'll talk."

Stifling a triumphant smile, he rose. "If you'll come with me, we'll go see my grandmother. She's in Amelia's suite. Technically it's not a nursery, but it's what we could do on short notice."

When Erin walked beside him to the open door, he realized in heels she was taller than most women he knew. He caught a faint scent of an exotic perfume that was enticing. Keenly aware of her, he motioned her ahead and she walked past him with a polite, "Thank you."

When she passed him, he couldn't keep from letting his gaze drift down her back and linger on her hips. There was a slight, appealing sway with each step she took, and he thoroughly enjoyed the walk to the baby's suite.

His grandmother, a tall, slender woman, stood in the center of the room holding Amelia. Strands of her gray-streaked brown hair had escaped the clip behind her head and a frown furrowed her brow. Her lavender blouse had come out of her slacks, adding to her disheveled appearance. Yet another reason to hire Erin instantly, Cade thought. His grandmother needed her rest.

Margo Wakely held her crying great-grandchild as she crossed the room. "Amelia is up from her nap and occasionally she doesn't wake easily."

"I'll take her," Cade said and instantly she handed Amelia to him. He spoke softly to his little niece while smoothing her pink jumper. Black curls framed her face and tears spilled from her big blue eyes. He kissed her lightly on the forehead while patting her back and talking softly to her for a minute before looking up.

"Grandmother, meet Luke's younger sister, Erin Dorsey. Erin, this is my grandmother Margo Wakely," he said, continuing to pat Amelia's back.

"I'm sorry for your loss, Mrs. Wakely," Erin said.

"Thank you. It's still difficult and so sad for Amelia."

"Here's our baby," Cade said, looking at Amelia who continued to cry. "Usually she's a sweetie who's happy." He shrugged. "This isn't good timing."

"I've had lots of experience with babies. Let me take her." She took Amelia from Cade and walked with her. In seconds Amelia quieted while Erin lightly patted her and walked back to Cade and his grandmother.

"Luke was right," Cade said, looking at her handling Amelia with more ease than his grandmother had and far more ease than he felt. "You're good with babies."

"With my younger siblings I've been around babies since I was two. But don't let a few minutes fool you. Sometimes they cry with me, too, although usually they don't cry a long time. Probably because I'm relaxed around them. Besides helping with my younger siblings, I did a lot of babysitting, helped with the nursery at church, that sort of thing." She looked down at Amelia, talking to her softly. "You're right—she's a sweetie."

Amelia babbled, reaching out a small fist to grab Erin's suit lapel and tug on it.

Erin picked up a pink rattle from toys spread on a nearby table and in seconds Amelia focused on the rattle. She took it in her chubby hand, making it spin and shake.

"She likes you," Margo said. "I haven't seen you in years, Erin. I remember one time when Cade left his books at your house and your brother drove over. I answered the door and you handed me his books while your brother waited in the car. You seemed a lot younger than Cade or Luke."

"I am younger. Eight years, to be exact," she replied and Cade was surprised because she was older than he had guessed.

"Now you're all grown up and a beautiful woman," Margo said, causing Erin to smile another dimpled smile that carried an impact Cade tried to resist.

"Thanks, Mrs. Wakely." She gazed down at Amelia who was happily playing with the rattle. "Look at those big, dark blue eyes. Such a beautiful little girl."

"I have to agree," Margo replied, smiling at Erin,

then casting a nod to Cade, as if giving him her seal of approval.

Cade wholeheartedly agreed. Erin was perfect for the job.

As she looked at Amelia, Cade's gaze raked over Erin. There was only one drawback. His attraction. There could be no flirting with her—something he never thought would be a problem where Luke's younger sister was concerned. And no kissing, he thought as he watched her full red lips graze Amelia's soft cheek. Talking to Luke last week, Cade had dismissed anything sexual between them. Now he realized he had probably never in his life been as wrong about something.

He just had to remember Luke was her brother. Other than his brothers, Luke was his best friend, and Cade was not about to jeopardize their long-standing relationship for a brief flirtation that would be forgotten when Erin left for grad school.

Not one bit. Telling himself he could do this, he cleared his throat and got the attention of the two women.

"Grandmother, we'll give Amelia back to you because Erin has limited time."

"Thanks for quieting her down," Margo said as she took the baby. "You have a nice touch and she likes you."

Erin smiled again. "She's a sweet and beautiful baby."

"She looks a lot like her father and she has a resemblance to her uncle," Margo said, smiling at Cade.

"Grandmother, I'll be back soon. Call Maisie if you need some help," Cade said, referring to his cook. He had already made arrangements for her to help his grandmother with Amelia when she needed it.

"I always call Maisie when I need her," Margo said.

As he walked with Erin into the hall he said, "Amelia sleeps through the night, but it's still a lot for Grandmother to take care of her. I try to be here as much as possible so I can take care of her in the evenings, but because of business, there are times I can't be at the ranch. I need a nanny as soon as possible. You saw both of us with her. I'm a novice and Grandmother has forgotten what she knew about childcare," he admitted.

"You'll learn what to do."

"It's scary. When Amelia cries, I feel like I'm failing her and Nate and Lydia."

"Relax a little, Cade. You take care of a lot of things on this ranch that are far more difficult and complicated. She's just a little girl."

"I meant it when I said that I don't know anything about babies or kids. And I especially don't know anything about little girls," he confessed. Then he rolled his eyes and let out a groan. "I can't bear to think of trying to deal with a teenage girl."

Erin laughed softly. "She won't be a teen for a few years so stop worrying about that. You'll get accustomed to Amelia in no time." Erin paused in the hallway to face him and her expression sobered. "I'm sorry I can't do this. While I'd love to take care of

Amelia and it would fit with my future career, living on your ranch or driving back and forth to my home in Dallas every day would be too much of a hardship. And I make a very good salary where I am. I wish you luck."

He looked into those deep green eyes that he knew he wouldn't forget for a long time and he knew what he had to do. "At least hear my offer before you turn me down."

He needed Erin. Amelia needed Erin. At the same time, he had known since she walked through his office door and he got his first sight of her, that resisting the urge to have her wouldn't be easy. But he hoped it would be possible. Besides, it was only a few months, not long enough to be much of a temptation.

"Come on," he said, turning toward his office and feeling her follow behind him. "Is there anyone you're seeing who'll be upset about you accepting a job on a ranch or being away from Dallas all week?" he asked as they walked.

"No, there isn't," she replied. "Luke leaves this week for the Antarctic and isn't scheduled to be back for the rest of the year. Mom is visiting her sister who lives in Arkansas—" She stopped, as if she suddenly thought of something. "I guess you weren't talking about my brother and family." She shook her head. "There's no man in my life."

"At the moment that works out better."

They entered Cade's office and sat in the leather chairs again. She crossed her legs and looked at him expectantly.

He placed his elbows on his knees and leaned closer. "I know you're capable and reliable. I know you and your family. I trust your credentials and I can trust you to care for Amelia like she was your own. You're perfect for this job."

"Thank you for such faith in me but—"

"I know. You don't think you'll make enough money for this nanny job to be worth your time. So, let's make it worth your time. It's five months counting December and then you'll leave for graduate school, right?"

"I'm quitting my job mid-December because I want to get ready to go to the university and I want a little time at home during Christmas."

"Okay. Only four months, plus two weeks, then. That makes a bigger salary even easier." When he paused to think, she waited quietly.

"Whatever your salary is for secretarial work, I'll quadruple it if you'll work for me," he offered.

Her eyes widened as she stared at him, saying nothing.

"You can have the use of one of my cars while you live here. That way you won't have wear and tear on your car or gas to buy when you come and go out here. You can have Saturdays and Sundays off after the first month and a ten-thousand-dollar signing bonus upon acceptance. The reason for asking you to stay on the weekends the first month is because everyone else is gone on the weekend. I'll get my cook to stay Saturday and take off one day during the week, but

I'm not ready to be alone with Amelia and have full charge of her care."

"Mercy…" As her lips parted, his attention was drawn to them and his curiosity rose over what it would be like to kiss her. It still shocked him that the same person he could so easily ignore as a kid now took his breath away, made his pulse race and inspired fantasies about hot kisses. He had to force his mind back onto his offer when she finally spoke.

"What you're offering is ridiculous," she whispered, still staring at him as if he had offered her all the gold in Fort Knox. "It's definitely something I have to consider, now that I'm going to grad school." Her gaze flickered as she said, "You know, if I hadn't known you all my life and if you weren't really close friends with my brother, I would suspect some ulterior motive for that kind of money. As it is, I know you well enough to know you're offering me the job for the right reasons."

"Yes, I am. Because I trust Luke's recommendation. And because Amelia is the highest priority in my life and I want the best nanny I can possibly get." He had to, for her and for his brother. When he was away from Amelia, he didn't want to worry about her. Or even when he was with her. Funny, he thought, how he could handle all kinds of things on his ranch, but taking care of a little baby scared the daylights out of him.

He looked at Erin and held his breath, hoping she wouldn't take a lot of time to make a decision.

She shook her head slowly and he wondered if she

intended to say no. He needed her desperately. If she turned him down, how much more should he offer to get her to accept the job?

"I don't need time. I can't possibly turn down your offer. When do you want me to start?"

Two

"As soon as you possibly can."

He felt relief surging in him and he could hardly stifle the smile that split his lips. Although temporary, he felt positive that he just hired an excellent nanny, and someone who could teach him how to be a parent so that later, he could select the best long-term nanny for his niece.

"I feel desperate and so does my grandmother, not to mention my cook who is doing some double shifts. Although sometimes I relieve her and cook for us so that she can help my grandmother," he explained. "Actually, tomorrow would be the best possible time for you to start, but I know you can't change your life that fast."

"No, I can't, but I can move to your ranch Monday

and get to know Amelia. If you or your grandmother can be here the first day or two, it would be nice, so I can see Amelia's routine and learn what I need to know about her."

"I'll work that out. Move in Monday and if I can help you, let me know. There are a lot of guys on this ranch willing to pitch in and help you move," he said. Every guy on the ranch would help once they got a glimpse of her. "I have a small plane and I also have a private jet I keep in Dallas. If you want, I can either have my pilot fly you here, because from the ranch it's a little over 160 miles to Dallas, or have someone pick you up in Dallas in a limo and move your things. From the ranch to Downly is twenty miles."

"My head is swimming. Let me think and I'll send you a text or call you later today. How's that?"

"That's excellent," he said, sitting back and smiling at her. She did look a bit overwhelmed.

"I'm stunned by your offer and am trying to adjust to the change in my life and what this job will mean to me," she said, her gaze shifting to his as she looked intently at him.

He became aware of how close they sat, her knees almost touching his, her exotic perfume filling the air. Her green eyes had darkened slightly and her rosy lips were turned up in a slight grin. He also became aware of how much he wanted to lean closer and taste them.

Would she always be such a temptation? he wondered. Or was it just the shock of seeing her looking so different, so mature, so feminine? He told himself he'd get used to the new Erin, with some time. Meanwhile, he had nothing to worry about where she was concerned. He had no qualms that she would be circumspect, professional, focused on Amelia.

He would, too, if he always kept in mind how vulnerable Erin was and how much she was into marriage, family and permanent commitment. Also, how much he valued her brother's friendship.

And she would never flirt with him or come on to him. He remembered how solemn she used to be. The reminder should be a reassurance to him, but for some reason it wasn't.

"When you're here, if you ever have any problems, don't hesitate to tell me," he said, his voice a deeper rasp.

"Thank you," she replied. "You know, I wouldn't do this if it weren't for your friendship with Luke and all the years we've known you."

"I wouldn't do this if it weren't for Luke, either," he said.

"And I doubt if I'll need any help, but I will let you know if I do. I don't even know what I need to bring."

"Let's go look at where you'll stay." He stood but paused as he exited his office. "One more thing," he said, "I'd like you to be on duty Friday nights. If you have some place you want to go on a Friday, let me know and I'll work around it, but on Fridays, I'd like to go out."

"That's fine. I think that would work out really well," she added and he smiled.

"Don't sound so happy to be rid of me," he said and she looked startled.

"I'm joking," he added swiftly, wanting to get back to being impersonal. "If you don't want to stay by yourself with Amelia, there are a couple of wives of the cowboys who work for me who live on the ranch. I can get them to stay on Friday night so you'll have someone else here with you."

"I'll be fine. They're all here on the ranch, so someone I can call won't be far away if necessary. Right?"

"Right. Come meet Maisie, my cook. She's still in the kitchen. She has a house here and her husband works for me, too. Harold, my butler, has a house on the ranch and his wife cooks for the people who work here." Cade took Erin's arm lightly to lead her out, and was surprised when the faint contact sent tingles up his arm. Yes, he thought, the woman was certainly tempting. Thank goodness once he had her situated and familiar with her charge and his staff, he could throw himself into work and see her less.

But how could he do that?

He needed to learn how to cope with Amelia. He needed to follow Erin around and see how to care for his charge. He also needed to bond with Amelia and when he did, Erin would be present, too. They were going to be thrown together, living together in his ranch house, spending a lot of time together with Amelia. And he had to remain cool and professional, the boss and his nanny.

He clung to the knowledge that even though Erin was gorgeous, there were other beautiful women who were far more lighthearted, ready to party, wanting the same freedom he did and who hadn't lost a baby or been hurt badly in a recent broken engagement. There were so many reasons to remain professional and distant with her, so why did they seemed to evaporate when he looked into her big, green eyes?

They entered the kitchen where a slender woman with braided blond hair wiped the countertops. "Ahh, hello, there," she said. "You must be Luke's younger sister. I can see a family resemblance."

Erin laughed. "I've heard that before, but not often."

"Erin, meet Maisie Elsworth, my cook and the person who keeps this place going. If you have questions about Amelia, the job or the ranch, or need help, Maisie is the person to ask."

"Absolutely," Maisie replied, smiling. "You'll love little Amelia and maybe you can teach this Wild West cowboy how to calm her. She's adorable." Maisie looked away and wiped her eyes, turning her back. "You'll have to give me a moment. I feel as if I lost one of my own boys when we lost Amelia's dad. The same for the little one's mother. So sad, and sometimes it hits me out of the blue," she said, still wiping her eyes.

Cade stepped up to put his arm around her and give her a squeeze. He stood quietly while she became composed again and turned to Erin.

"Sorry," Maisie said. "Moments come without warning when I realize they're gone forever and I think of little Amelia."

"Don't ever apologize because you love someone,"

Erin said. Cade thought about her miscarriage and
how much she must have hurt over losing her baby,
and how much she was still hurting.

"Ahh, you'll be a good nanny for our little baby,"
Maisie told her. "I hope your brother is fine. I miss
seeing him. They were fun boys, but now they're
grown men and busy and I don't see them."

"You see me plenty, Maisie," Cade said with a
grin. "You'll see more of me today, but right now, I
want to show Erin where she'll be staying when she
moves in."

"It'll be good to have you with us," she said to Erin
and Cade wondered whether he had just complicated
his future while making Amelia's more secure.

Next, Cade took Erin to a suite that held four
rooms. She walked into the center of the living area,
turning to look at the room that had oak floors, a thick
area rug in two tones of blue, watercolor paintings
of horses on the walls, and glass and teak furniture.

Cade watched her turn to look around, his gaze
running over her. He was still amazed by the changes
in her appearance, even though common sense told
him she wouldn't look the way she had at ten.

"Go ahead and look at the bedroom, the closet and
the adjoining bathroom," Cade urged, wanting her
to be happy with the job and where she would live.
"There's also a small office with computer equip-
ment."

He watched her thick red hair swing slightly across
her shoulders as she walked out of sight into the bedroom. When she returned, she smiled—another

friendly, dimpled smile that under other circumstances he would have accepted as an invitation to flirt.

"This is marvelous," she said. "I'll go back to the office and give notice today. They won't mind letting me go because I'm temporary anyway. I'll just leave sooner than I had planned."

He suspected they were going to mind letting her go, but he merely nodded. "Good. We'll stop by my office and I'll write a check to you for your signing bonus." They fell into step and he was aware of her close beside him. When they entered his office he hastily wrote the check, his fingers brushing hers when he handed it to her.

Every physical contact, no matter how slight or how much he tried to ignore it, was noticeable—all red flag warnings that he would have to deal carefully with her.

What made the feathery brushes of their hands noticeable besides his reaction was awareness that she responded, too. Her reaction showed in tiny ways: a surprised look, a flicker in her eyes, a deep breath. Some kind of chemistry existed between them, an attraction that he could not pursue and she didn't want.

When they walked to his front porch, she turned to face him, offering her hand.

"Thank you for this fantastic offer. I'm going to love taking care of Amelia and now I won't have to worry about finances so much," she said, withdrawing her hand that was soft and slender.

"Even though you're on a full scholarship, I know

your brother has offered to pay your college expenses and you've always turned him down."

"He put himself through school and I want to do this on my own, too, the way he did. I have my undergraduate degree now, so I'm making progress and I see the proverbial light at the end of the tunnel."

"Congratulations. That's commendable," Cade said, realizing she had a streak of independence that was so like her brother. "For the present, you have my phone number in case you need anything. And the offer of help to move still stands. I'll see you Monday."

"Thanks. I never dreamed I'd be in a business arrangement with you someday. And I'm sure you wouldn't have thought it possible to be in one with me," she said, her eyes twinkling. "I might as well have been wallpaper for all the attention you ever gave me back then."

He smiled and held back a reply that came to mind instantly, that he definitely noticed her now and she wasn't anything like wallpaper. He glanced at her full lips and wondered again about kissing her. More forbidden thoughts plagued him, thoughts that he would have to squelch. How many times would he have to remind himself?

"Cade, thank you again so very much for this job. I'm thrilled and looking forward to getting started," she said.

With an effort, he stepped back. "See you Monday," he said, taking a deep breath.

"Sure," she said, giving him one more long look

before she hurried to her small black car. She waved as she drove away.

He had an excellent, trustworthy nanny—and a nagging worry that he might be bringing trouble home in a big way. Was he going to be able to ignore the chemistry that smoldered between them today? Was he going to be careful to avoid trying to seduce his nanny? He had to or he'd lose his best friend forever. Besides, he wasn't interested in commitment and Erin was the marrying kind. She had already been hurt badly and was vulnerable. He couldn't hurt her more.

Cade watched her car go down the ranch drive, but all he really saw were big green eyes and a rosy mouth that looked ripe for kissing.

When Erin glanced at her rearview mirror, Cade still stood on the porch of his sprawling ranch house. A tall Texas rancher, a man worth millions, yet he looked like other cowboys from ranches all over Texas. Except he was more handsome than most.

Smiling, she thought about how he had been shocked that she had grown up. He had never paid attention to her the years he was in high school. All her brother's friends had seemed big and intimidating and they had seldom taken notice of her, which was a relief to her. She just tried to avoid them and go ahead with what she wanted to do.

By the time Cade graduated from college, she was in her early teens and was attracted to him, thinking he was to-die-for handsome. She had a silly, schoolgirl crush that she told no one about. She knew the times he was at their house he didn't notice her any more than he had when she was nine years old and he had been in high school.

She hadn't seen Cade in years and it was a surprise to see an appealing, good-looking rancher. A grown man now—handsome, filled out and older, with that air of confidence that was as evident as it was with her brother.

Even though Cade was still her brother's closest friend, there was only a little she knew about him.

When she rounded a bend in the road and his house disappeared from the view behind her, she let out her breath. With the check he had just given her, there was no way she could turn down his job offer, but it was going to hurt badly at times.

She still wasn't over her losses completely, though the pain had eased somewhat. Losing her baby had been devastating and when Cade handed Amelia to her, she'd had a terrible clutch to her heart and felt tears sting her eyes. As she drove down the graveled, dusty ranch road, a pang still tore at her. She didn't think she would ever stop hurting over losing her baby, even though it had been early in her pregnancy, and she knew that Amelia was going to be a constant reminder of what she had lost.

Now she had taken a job that was going to dredge up that pain again every day until she got accustomed to dealing with Amelia and could focus on her charge without thinking about her miscarriage.

Amelia looked so adorable, she should bring cheer just by being a sweet baby.

Cade, however, might not be so easily handled. He loomed, another giant difficulty because of his incredible appeal. What might make working for him difficult was the chemistry between them. Where had that come from? She felt it and she knew he had. Or maybe he stirred that reaction in all the women he met.

Several times today, he had looked at her intently, giving her the look a man gives a woman when he actually sees her as an attractive woman. She wasn't so out of practice that she didn't recognize it.

It wouldn't have mattered if he had spent the whole interview flirting with her. She didn't want to date, didn't want to fall in love, didn't want any kind of relationship. The pain of her broken engagement was still too real, too intense. The consequences of any relationship would bring back too many hurtful memories.

She didn't want to get involved emotionally with any man at this point in her life and definitely not Cade. She knew his views on relationships and his cynical view of marriage. She might not ever be able to have a baby, but she still wanted marriage and children in her future and that was not what Cade had ever wanted. If she could resist Cade's appeal and deal with the hurt and reminders of her loss that Amelia would unknowingly cause, this job would be great. A huge windfall for her, and good experience for her future career. Cade's offer had been irresistible. No way could she have turned it down.

Even though Erin tried to avoid thinking too much about her doctor's warning that she might not ever be able to carry a baby full-term, it was impossible to forget. If she couldn't bear a child, she would adopt. She would have a family, one way or another, but that would come in her future. Now she intended to concentrate on grad school and her career.

For a few months she would take care of a precious little girl. Amelia Callahan was a beautiful baby with lots of thick black curls and big dark blue eyes like her uncle. Erin remembered the few minutes when she held her and Amelia had stopped crying, looking into Erin's eyes as if they were bonding.

And you bonded with her uncle, too.

She ignored the insinuating voice inside her head. She hadn't bonded with Cade; she'd simply looked at him while he spoke to her. Yeah, and drowned in his eyes. And nearly ignited when he touched her.

Who was she kidding? Working for Cade was going to take difficult to new levels.

Living on the ranch, she could only hope Cade would be gone most of the day. It would make her job easier if he wasn't around. She was going to love precious little Amelia and when December came, it would be dreadful to say goodbye.

In the meantime she'd simply avoid caring too much about Amelia's appealing guardian.

On Monday Erin changed clothes several times, finally deciding on practical navy slacks, a short-sleeve matching cotton blouse with a round neckline and navy pumps. She brushed her hair and stood looking at herself until she realized she was thinking about how Cade would view her. She had to stop that. And she had to put a halt to the heart-pounding, prickly awareness of him that had plagued her all weekend.

Her apartment bell buzzed and she went to the intercom to hear her brother's voice. "Am I too early?"

"No. I'm ready to go. Come up."

She opened her apartment door and in minutes Luke swept into the room. "Hey, you look nice," he said, studying her and then turning his eyes on her bags, laptop, carry-on and purse stacked near the door.

"Thanks, Luke, for helping me load my car."

"Sure. I'm glad you're doing this and I'm glad he's paying you well. I figured he would."

"The pay is fantastic. Now I don't have to worry about school."

"I still say, anytime you need anything or if you run short of money, let me know. I'm single, earning a good living and I'll be happy to help you. You don't have to pay me back, either—that's the best part."

She smiled at him. "The best part is that you made the offer. That gives me a secure feeling that I can always turn to you if something disastrous happens."

"Damn straight. Speaking of something disastrous… Let me remind you again—"

"Luke," she cautioned and laughed. "Don't tell me to avoid going out with Cade. He never even noticed me until he wanted to hire me. He knows I'm your little sister and he won't jeopardize his friendship with you. Now stop worrying about me."

"I'm worrying about what Cade will do, although I don't think he'll hit on you for the reasons you just gave. I can promise that he notices you now. He didn't when you were eight or nine years old, but…well, you look a lot different now. Let me remind you that while Cade loves the ladies, he is dead set against marriage. When it comes to long-term relationships, there's not a serious bone in his body. He doesn't know what a real family is—I know he always enjoyed being at our house partly because of our parents. He's close with his brothers and his mother had good intentions, but she was more interested in a social life. What I'm saying is Cade is not your type and you don't need another hurt."

"Luke—"

"Be advised. I will come back from Antarctica and punch him out if he tries to date you," he said, grinning at her.

She laughed, shaking her head and not taking him seriously. "No, you won't. He's your lifelong best friend. I think that covers it all. He knows how you feel and he knows I'm your little sister. I'm going to be the nanny. I'll be with his grandmother and his little ward, but I won't be with him. Frankly, I think he's scared to take care of Amelia by himself and he doesn't know how."

"You've got that right. For once in his life he is terrified. He told me as much when I spoke to him. He doesn't know anything about babies, even though he had younger brothers. They're too close in age for him to have learned anything about babies. Oh, and speaking of his brothers… Little brother Gabe Callahan is single, closer to your age, likes to party and I imagine he'll ask you out. And Gabe doesn't take anything seriously—definitely not a relationship."

"Duly noted," she said, laughing at her brother. "If I get asked out, I can deal with that, and since I'll be the nanny and Cade is desperate and doesn't know how to care for Amelia, I'll have the best possible excuse to turn down any invitations by any guys I meet. Cade's already asked me if I would stay on Friday nights so he can go out. Stop worrying."

"Okay," he said, though she got the impression he really wanted to continue his dire warnings.

"Let's get the car loaded before I'm late arriving at his ranch. I'll text you and keep you posted on how I'm getting along. Everyone you work with there will wonder why you keep getting reports from me on my well-being."

"They'll know it's because I can't be there myself and I'm a class-A worrier when it comes to my baby sister. Cade is a great guy and my best friend, but I don't want you hurt by him."

"Luke, for the last time, you've got to stop. I believe you're the one who wanted me to interview with him and go to work for him," she said sweetly and Luke clamped his mouth shut. "Let's go," she said, picking up a bag which he took from her hands.

After her car was packed and her apartment locked, she hugged Luke. "I hope you love your work.

You know, environmental engineers can find jobs in Texas."

He grinned. "This is a change and I'll learn new things. The South Pole needs protection. They have wastewater problems just like Dallas does."

"Don't give me one of your lectures about protecting our earth. I'm recycling."

"Keep at it. Every little bit helps. For my part, I'm excited about working there."

"Good. I'm excited about my new job, too. Amelia is a precious little girl."

Her brother studied her. "You'll work there a little over four months—you shouldn't get too attached in that time."

She brushed off his concern. "That little girl needs someone to care for her and I'm happy to get the job—and very happy to get the money," she added lightly. But inside, she was afraid she was already attached to Amelia, yet willing to care for her because her guardian was clueless about baby care. "It's too short a time for any attachment I form to get too strong," she lied. "Now you stop worrying and take care of yourself." She hugged him again.

"Don't I always?" Luke grinned as he held open the car door for her to get behind the wheel. He closed her door and stepped back, and she saw him watching her as she drove away. She turned the corner and he was lost to sight, but his warnings about Cade echoed in her mind.

Would this job be the blessing for all as she hoped? Or was she driving straight into trouble and more heartache?

* * *

When Erin arrived at the ranch, Cade came out in long strides to greet her. Her heartbeat jumped. This wasn't going to be the easiest job, she realized right away. The instant she saw him all her intentions to resist Cade's appeal vanished like smoke in the wind.

August sunshine spilled over him, and locks of his raven hair blew slightly in the breeze. Emitting a contagious vitality, he looked tan, strong and fit in his tight jeans, boots, and a red plaid shirt with the sleeves rolled up.

"Welcome to the ranch," he said, smiling at her. "My grandmother is thrilled about your arrival today. Frankly, she's not accustomed to caring for a baby and she's worn threadbare."

Erin smiled at him, aware of his dark blue eyes as his gaze swept over her. If he had stayed in Dallas where he worked with his younger brother Gabe, in commercial real estate, and left her with his grandmother, Maisie, Harold and the rest of his staff, her life would be peaceful. As it was, while she looked up at such blue eyes and thick, black hair, she wondered if she would have another peaceful moment until this job ended in December.

"I'm eager to get started and to get to know Amelia," she said, trying to focus on her job.

Cade shouldered a carry-on and took her laptop from her hands. Their hands brushed in a casual touch that stirred more sparks.

"We'll get all your things," he said as Harold came out of the house and hurried to carry her luggage.

Holding Amelia in her arms, his grandmother stepped out and stood watching on the porch while Erin made her way up the walk, Cade beside her. At the top of the steps, she paused to greet Margo and Amelia.

"I'm so happy you're here," Margo said.

She returned the pleasantry. "Let me take Amelia," she said once she entered the house and set down her purse. Dressed in a blue-and-yellow jumper and yellow blouse, Amelia smelled sweet. When she studied Erin with her thickly lashed big blue eyes, Erin smiled at her.

"I'm glad you're here so you can tell me about her routine," Erin said quietly to Margo.

"We haven't exactly established a routine. It's been a long, long time since I've had the care of a baby. I had two girls and Crystal was my youngest. She's Cade's mother. By the time the boys were born, Crystal had a nanny and help, so there was little for me to do about their care. They're close together in age and I didn't raise boys, so I didn't really have them with me often."

Erin nodded, thinking how different that was from her mother's life and her own, caring for her little nephews who stayed with her parents for a lot of nights. Her parents had raised a big family with boys and girls and they loved having their grandchildren around.

"We'll go to what is the nursery for now," Cade said. "Amelia's suite is between my suite and yours. The sitting room is now a playroom. Like I said earlier, we really didn't have time to change things when I got Amelia. I wanted to get her settled and familiar with where she is. I think she needs stability after the upheaval in her life." He clamped his mouth closed and a muscle flexed in his jaw. She guessed he was having a bad moment about losing his brother and sister-in-law, or possibly a bad moment thinking about Amelia losing a mommy and daddy. She could understand because of her own heartaches and she looked at Amelia, smoothing the baby's unruly curls from her forehead.

Big blue eyes studied her solemnly and Erin smiled at Amelia, knowing the baby would grow accustomed to her as time passed.

She glanced at Cade to find him watching her and she wondered what he was thinking. But she didn't ask.

Cade paused in front of Amelia's suite and motioned her in, though he moved down toward another open door.

"I'll put these in your room and be right in."

Erin entered the baby's suite and turned to see Margo settle on a sofa. She glanced around at a room she had barely looked at the day of her interview. Stuffed toys were scattered on a blanket on the floor. There were more on a chair, plus rattles and blocks. A toy box overflowed with baby toys on one side of the sofa. There was a baby swing at one side of the room and a baby chair in the middle of the room.

Erin sat in a rocker and rocked while still holding Amelia. "She doesn't seem interested in getting down or in her toys."

"She woke early this morning, so she might be getting sleepy again," Margo said. "Cade is here with you and if you don't have any questions, I think I'll go answer my emails. Call me if you need me," she added and Erin nodded, wondering if she was going to be alone with Cade often or if he would disappear to work. Whatever happened, she realized her job as nanny had started instantly and she wasn't going to get any schedule from Margo regarding Amelia.

Getting down on the floor with Amelia, Erin rolled a clear plastic ball filled with sparkling objects and little silver bells. As she looked at the pretty little girl, she knew she was in for another heartache because she was going to love this baby so much by the time she finished her temporary job. Amelia was easy to love. Maybe she found reassurance from those who were taking care of her. Whatever made Amelia happy, Erin was drawn to her. In almost four months, she was certain she would love the girl as her own, but she would let her go because that would be best for Amelia.

If only she could guard her heart from falling in love with the handsome rancher who was Amelia's guardian. How was she going to resist him when they had to be together for Amelia's sake? How was she going to resist him, too, when he already made her heart pound and she wanted to be in his arms?

Cade entered the nursery and saw Erin on a blanket on the floor rolling a ball around in front of Amelia, while Amelia laughed and grabbed for it.

When Erin looked up at him, her red hair swung

across her shoulders and he drew a deep breath. Why hadn't Luke told him his sister had grown into such a beauty?

He knew exactly why and he needed to remember that he had promised Luke he would not do anything to hurt Erin. As he gazed into her green eyes, he tried to remember what he had intended to tell her.

"Ah, Erin, I see Grandmother has already fled the scene and left it all to you," he said, looking down at her and looking at Amelia. "Amelia seems happy."

"For having such upheaval in her life, she's a happy baby. I think they sense what's happening around them."

He sat on the end of the sofa, so close he could easily reach out and touch her and Amelia. "She's doing better," he said as he shifted his attention to the baby. "At first she cried a lot. Thank goodness she doesn't cry as much now because that tears me up. When she's been fed and isn't sleepy and everything should be all right, but she still cries, I feel as if she wants Lydia or Nate."

"Cade, I'm sorry," Erin said softly, touching his hand lightly. She removed her hand instantly and drew a deep breath as he turned to look at her.

The moment had changed again as soon as she'd touched him. He was instantly hot, wanting to reach for her, wanting to flirt with her, to kiss her. That slight touch that was simply meant to console him stirred a potent desire within him.

Wide-eyed, Erin looked at him, then shifted away. When her cheeks turned pink, he decided she felt the same rush of desire as he had—and the knowledge only deepened his response to her.

"Amelia's happy now," she said, casting her gaze on the baby rolling the ball around. Erin laughed as she caught the ball and placed it back in front of Amelia.

"Now that you're here, my grandmother will be going home to Dallas."

"That's fine. You've hired me and I can manage. That's my job."

"I know you can take care of her easily, but I really expected Grandmother to at least give you a day. But I should have known because I know my grandmother. She's not into childcare."

"Your grandmother has been here since the accident?"

He shook his head. "No. Last May my older brother—actually my half brother—Blake Callahan married. His wife, Sierra, is expecting. She's been so good—she took Amelia for a week when I couldn't right after the accident in June. I didn't want to impose on her, but she insisted."

"That was nice of her," she said, smiling at him and turning back to Amelia. His gaze ran over Erin's profile and he noticed her dark lashes were long and thick. Her skin was flawless, soft looking. He realized the drift of his thoughts and tried to refocus. He told her more about his new sister-in-law.

"Sierra is like you are with Amelia, totally relaxed and competent with a baby. She has a big family with lots of kids. Her grandfather was involved in an agency in Kansas City that had a shelter for the home-less. They've branched out and have a home for kids who need a place, and this past year they opened a small animal rescue."

"I hope I get to meet her."

"You probably will because I'm close with Blake. Sierra's family is the opposite of ours. My dad, Dirkson Callahan, is not into family and kids. He attended the funeral, left when it was over and we haven't seen him since. He's too busy making money."

"I've known you a long time, but I don't know your family."

"My dad is Dirkson Callahan and his first marriage was only eight months long, no children. He married Veronica next and had Blake, but divorced when Blake was a baby. He never acknowledged Blake, not until recently when Blake contacted him. Then my dad married my mom, Crystal, and I'm the oldest, then Nate and then Gabe. After Mom and Dad divorced he hasn't married again, but there were plenty of mistresses."

"You make me more grateful than ever for my parents."

"You're lucky. Anyway, when Nate's will was read, I was named guardian, but I already knew that because Nate asked me before they did their wills and set up a trust. Nate and I were always close. Anyway, Grandmother took pity on me and came to help me until I could get a nanny. And Maisie was around to help out, of course."

"It sounds to me as if you've had everything covered."

"I want everything perfect for Amelia. I owe it to Nate and Lydia." He reached out and cradled the baby's cheek before she grabbed her ball again. "Amelia seems fragile. I don't know whether she likes me, I don't know what to feed her. I'm at a loss," he admitted. "I've never felt so helpless."

"Now I'm here for her, and before I leave you can hire another nanny and you'll be fine. So will Amelia because you love her. Don't worry, Cade, I'll teach you how to care for her."

He bit back a reply that she could teach him a lot of things, but he wouldn't have been referring to Amelia.

"There's one rule of thumb when it comes to babies," she said. "Use common sense." Her eyes seemed to twinkle when she added, "You run this ranch and it's loaded with babies, just the four-footed kind."

"They're easy and that's different. I think you're on the verge of laughing at me," he said, looking into those green eyes that captivated him.

"Not really. You're worrying too much. She's going to love you. I've already seen her reach for you, so she likes you and trusts you or she wouldn't do that."

"I hope so," he said. "Look, I know Grandmother abandoned you but I have to make a long-distance call. Then I'll come back."

"You don't need to come back—not that I don't want to see you, but we'll get along fine."

"Can I get anything for you right now?"

"No. We're fine. We'll get to know each other. She'll probably take a nap later."

"I do know she had lunch before you came because I fed her. Don't hesitate to go get my grandmother if you need to. She shouldn't have left you the first hour you're here. Or go ask Maisie. She's polite and honest. And you can always call me on my cell if you need me."

"This isn't a difficult job," she said, smiling at him. "Go do what you have to do," she said, rolling the ball back and forth in front of Amelia who patted it and tried unsuccessfully to grab it. Erin glanced up to meet Cade's solemn gaze and the moment she looked into his eyes, he felt fiery sparks between them.

Unfortunately—or maybe fortunately—he needed to get some business taken care of, so he had to leave her. He suspected the better he got to know Erin, the more difficult it was going to be to keep a professional attitude with her. And he had to.

No matter if it killed him.

Only when Cade left the room did Erin let out the breath she'd been holding. How on earth was she going to get through the next few months when desire arced between them like that? Though the two times she'd been with him had been relatively brief, this heart-pounding, breathtaking fiery attraction had flared to life each time. It was as unnerving as it was unwanted. She was certain it would disappear and nothing would come of it, but until that happened, his appeal shocked her.

Amelia gave the big ball a push and it rolled away. She held out her tiny arms and waved them, wanting the ball back. Laughing, Erin got it and rolled it to Amelia. "Here's your pretty ball, sweet baby," she said softly, wanting Amelia to get accustomed to being with her.

This job wasn't really that different from the many she'd had as a babysitter except she would live on the ranch for the next few months. Living on his ranch with Cade—that was the difference. She had felt sorry for his hurt and wasn't thinking beyond sympathy for him and for little Amelia when she had placed her hand on Cade's as a reassurance.

The instant she'd touched him, everything had changed. Her sympathy vanished, replaced by a fiery awareness of Cade as an appealing, sexy man. The contact made her tingle; even more, the slight touch of her hand on his had made her want to be in his arms.

She hadn't felt a shred of desire for any man since she'd had the miscarriage last year. After Adam broke their engagement and called off the wedding, even the tiniest flicker of desire was gone. She hadn't wanted to date. No man had appealed to her. She had thrown herself into school and been numb otherwise.

That had ended the minute she walked into Cade Callahan's office and looked into his dark blue eyes. That strong physical awareness didn't diminish, even though she knew all about Cade's attitude toward commitment and his decision never to marry. She knew he liked to party and liked women who wanted to party. He was definitely not the type of man she would ever want to get involved with. Intimacy with Cade, however spectacular physically, would be meaningless emotionally.

So why did she have this volatile reaction to a mere look from him, or these tingles from an accidental contact of their hands or arms? He hadn't flirted or tried to kiss her, yet the slightest brush of their hands made her heart thud and made her want to be in his arms, to have his mouth on hers.

How could she have this reaction to a man her brother had repeatedly warned her didn't have it in him to be serious or to place any value on marriage and family?

How could she be drawn to a man like that?

She had to get more resistance to Cade and keep up her guard because she was going to be in close contact with him. They would have physical contact. They were sharing a baby and they would be sharing a house. Both their rooms opened into Amelia's room.

Luke had warned her and he was right. She did not want to go home with a broken heart when this job ended no more than her brother wanted her to. But she had a problem. A big problem. How was she going to resist Cade, a man she had been attracted to since she was thirteen, a man who could make her tremble by a look and make her want him by the mere brush of his fingers? How could she stay under the same roof, day and night, and say no to him?

Three

After playing for almost an hour with Amelia, Erin realized Amelia was tired and picked her up to change her and rock her to sleep. Leaving the door open between rooms, she unpacked her things.

That night for dinner they ate in the casual dining area adjoining the kitchen on one side. There was a large casual living area on the other side. Both areas were separated from the kitchen by islands, and there was a lot of space in all three rooms.

During dinner with Margo and Cade, Erin's attention was on Amelia, although she was well aware of Cade. After dinner they moved to a sunny living area that overlooked part of the patio and flower beds of multicolored blooms surrounded by a green lawn.

The house and lawn were an oasis in miles of mesquite and cacti.

Later when Erin left to put Amelia down for the night, Margo went with her. Leaving the task to Erin, Margo hovered in the background, sitting in one of the large recliners in the baby's room until Erin stopped rocking Amelia. Erin put her down and stood beside her to make sure she stayed asleep. Finally, as they tiptoed out of the baby's suite, Margo turned to Erin.

"Thank you for taking her today. I knew you would do fine and it's an immense relief."

"I enjoyed taking care of her. She's a sweet, happy little girl."

"Well, I'm not as young as I was and I'm really worn-out from childcare. I'm going to turn in early so I'll say good-night now. But you go join Cade. There's a baby monitor in Amelia's room and you can hear it anywhere in the house so you'll know if she stirs. You can see her, too, with this iPad that Cade bought for this purpose. You've been a great help today, Erin. I'm thankful you took this job and Cade is relieved, too, that you're here. It's wonderful to turn Amelia's care over to someone who likes her and knows how to take care of babies."

"Thank you," Erin said, hating to tell Margo goodnight and go back to Cade when it was only the two of them. Reminding herself of his polite attitude earlier in the day, she parted with Margo, took a deep breath and left to join him.

As she entered the room, he stood, his gaze sweeping over her and, again, her fragile peace of mind shattered. When he had come in from work, he had showered and changed to fresh jeans and a blue knit shirt. Locks of his unruly wavy hair fell slightly on his forehead. Standing quietly, he dominated the room and made her pulse quicken, a reaction she wished she didn't have. Cade was too handsome, too appealing and she was thankful he had been professional and polite so far, because she wasn't ready to deal with him otherwise.

As she glanced around the room that had comfortable furniture, soft lighting and an inviting casualness, she noticed Amelia's toys had vanished, probably to her toy box.

"Thank you. You picked up her toys and put them away. Very nice, Cade, but I'll always be happy to do that. It goes with my job."

"Not necessarily," he said easily. "I'm able-bodied and can pick up toys. Also, congratulations. You made it through your first day. Want a glass of wine to celebrate?"

Smiling, she shook her head. "Instead, I think a glass of iced tea will do nicely." She followed him to the bar. "It was a good day," she said as he poured her drink and held it out to her. When she took it from him, their fingers brushed, another casual bit of contact that should have gone unnoticed, but instead only heightened her smoldering awareness of him. She intended to drink some of her tea, stay about half an hour and then go to her suite.

"Let's sit where it's comfortable," he said, grabbing himself a beer and moving to a brown leather chair, while she sat in a tan wing chair. "Anything new from your brother except warnings about me?"

"Not really. Since we graduated from high school each one of us goes on with life. Chunks of time pass between communications with him and once he leaves, I don't expect to hear much from him."

"That may be a good thing." Cade smiled and she laughed, her dimple showing.

"You know my brother well. Luke's the oldest, so he's accustomed to telling the others what to do. I'm the next, and even though I'm twenty-two and there are several years between our ages, we're close. It's a little amazing you're such good friends because you're both alpha males—very much alike probably."

"We don't see each other as much now and we never did run each other's lives." He hesitated, then added, "Well, we both make suggestions, like him telling me to hire you."

"I imagine a better description would be *hounding* you to hire me until you were desperate enough to listen to him."

He smiled and her heart did another skip because it softened his features and it heightened his appeal.

"No," he replied. "I had mixed feelings about it until I saw you with Amelia. She took to you instantly and you were relaxed with her. Actually, anyone watching you who didn't know, would think you had been taking care of Amelia for a long time."

"I've spent a lot of time with babies."

"Well, Grandmother and I are grateful you've

adjusted so quickly. She's worn-out. I don't know whether she told you or not, she's going home tomorrow."

Erin drew a sharp breath. "I thought she planned to stay awhile after I arrived," she said, instantly thinking of the moments she would be alone with Cade.

"Not anymore. She said you don't seem to need anyone, that you took charge from the first moment and she's just watched." His eyes narrowed. "Is there some reason you feel she needs to stay longer?"

His blue eyes were intent and she didn't want him to realize how on edge she felt with him. He might guess why she didn't want his grandmother to go.

"No, of course not." She hoped she sounded positive and casual. "I'll be fine. I just didn't want her to feel unwanted."

He stared at her a moment in silence and then shook his head. "Believe me, she doesn't feel unwanted. She couldn't wait to turn Amelia's care over to you."

Erin smiled at him. "I'm happy to have full charge of Amelia. She's easy."

"You'll be great with Amelia." He looked away with a muscle working in his jaw and she guessed that he was thinking about his deceased brother.

He sipped his beer and turned to look at her again. "When I'm out on the ranch, you can always get me on my phone and don't hesitate if you need me. I'll introduce you to my foreman and you can call him, too. Maisie is here during the day and you can get her if you need help. There will always be someone close."

"That's good to know."

"I promised you a complete tour of the house—want to look now?"

"Yes. This is a good time," she said, standing. She had the feeling that he was carefully trying to be friendly and yet keep a distance, which was a relief.

He showed her the formal, grand living area with elegant furniture and a massive stone fireplace with a large watercolor landscape above the marble mantel. She was relieved to see the fireplace had padding to protect Amelia if she fell against the stone hearth.

The open area had thick, handcrafted area rugs and columns that separated it from the dining room which was dominated by a polished cherrywood table that would seat twenty-four.

"Do you actually have this many people here for dinner?" she said, looking at the elegant table and then turning to catch him gazing at her with an intense look as personal as the touch of his hand, and made her forget his dining room.

"Occasionally," he answered. His voice held a husky note and she walked into the hall.

"Where do we go from here?"

He followed in silence, a brooding look on his face. Was he regretting hiring her? She didn't think the look he gave her was one of regret. Far from it.

They toured his house while conversation remained polite, impersonal, and she kept a discreet distance between them. In the entertainment room, she turned to him. "Amelia is a sound sleeper. I think I'll look in on her and turn in myself."

"Sure," he said, walking beside her. "I told you earlier that my suite is on the other side of hers. Come look. I'll show you," he said and in a few minutes ushered her through a wide-open door into a big sitting room with floor-to-ceiling windows along one side of the room that led to a patio and yard. The sitting room had a large Navajo rug, a polished hardwood floor, a beamed twelve-foot ceiling and a giant television screen on one wall. Bookcases lined another wall and a stone fireplace was on the fourth wall. He'd decorated with oil paintings of landscapes and Western scenes.

"Come on and see my bedroom," he said, taking her arm lightly and going through another open door into a spacious bedroom with another fireplace, more bookshelves, more glass. His oversize king bed with navy and light blue as a color theme, as well as his large leather sofa added to a room that appeared comfortable and a reflection of the man who lived in it. Through open doors, she could see a bathroom and to another side she saw a door open to an office with three computer screens on a wide glass desk. She was aware it was his room, more aware of him standing close beside her.

"I have baby monitors in here, plus my iPad so I can see and hear her if she stirs."

"So if she cries both of us are going to see about her?" she asked, wanting to avoid any such thing.

"No, I'm leaving that for you. It's in an emergency that I'll be around."

Relieved, she nodded. "You have a beautiful house. Lots of room for little Amelia."

When they stepped into the hall, she smiled at him. "I have some of my things to put away. I didn't finish today and I want to check on Amelia, so I'll say good-night now."

"Good night, Erin. I can't tell you how glad we are to have you here," he said.

She nodded and turned, going into her suite when she really wanted to stay and talk, but knowing which was the wiser course to follow.

Before she went to bed, she had on her blue cotton robe over matching pajamas. She opened the connecting door to Amelia's big room and looked around. Seeing no other occupant, Erin crossed the room to Amelia's crib. Amelia lay curled on her side, her black ringlets tangled and her dark lashes casting shadows on her rosy cheeks. Erin paused beside her bed and a tight pain squeezed her heart.

What would her baby have been like? How many times would she wonder about that? How long would this big empty void be in her life? How long would the hurt of losing her little baby continue?

There were times she couldn't stop the tears and her loss overwhelmed her. As time passed, her tears came less often, but she didn't think they would ever stop. The loss was too big and too important.

She heard a faint scrape and looked around. The door to Cade's room was closed and he was probably moving around in his suite. She needed to get back to her own suite.

Smoothing ringlets off the baby's forehead, Erin thought about Amelia's loss she would cry over when she was old enough to understand, but right now she slept in blissful peace, too young to know she had lost both mother and father, secure in the love of Cade and Margo and the people around her.

Erin wiped away her tears again and inhaled deeply. She had a wonderful temporary job that would pay her a small fortune. She worked with a sweet baby and very nice people. If she could keep from falling in love with Cade and giving her heart to Amelia as well, she would have a wonderful experience.

How simple it sounded—resist falling in love with Cade, and avoid loving Amelia, too. Would it really be that easy when they would be together daily?

It was midafternoon by the time Erin saw Cade the next day. He was standing beside his grandmother on the front porch, a limo waiting to take her to his private jet in Dallas.

Erin watched while Margo hugged and kissed Amelia, who in turn smiled at her great-grandmother. Once again she was struck by the resemblance to Cade. They looked so much alike, Amelia could have been his baby. Obviously Cade and his brother resembled each other. She had never met any of his brothers, at least that she could recall, although they might have been at her house at one time or another.

Margo was dressed in yellow linen slacks and a matching blouse and pumps. Coincidentally, Erin had dressed Amelia in a yellow jumper and white blouse.

To say goodbye Erin had fastened a little yellow hair bow in Amelia's black curls. Erin didn't expect the ribbon to last long, but at least long enough for her to take several pictures of Margo holding Amelia.

When she handed Amelia to Erin, she smiled. "I'm glad you're taking pictures. Cade never thinks about it and neither do I, so we don't have recent pictures of her. Please send some to me."

"I'll send you copies of all I take," Erin replied.

"Amelia is going to love you like one of the family," Margo said as she patted her arm. "You can do much better than I can for this delightful girl."

"I don't know about that," Erin said politely, smiling at Margo. "But I agree she's a joy."

"She is, but at my age she's also a handful. I'm glad you're here. Now I won't worry about Cade or Amelia. You take care."

"I will," Erin answered, aware of Cade patiently waiting and watching them. When Margo turned away, he held her arm lightly to walk down the steps with her, to kiss her cheek and help her into the limo. He stood watching it drive away and then came back to the porch.

"They'll get her on the plane and she has a friend picking her up when she lands. She is so happy you're here and you're so competent."

Erin smiled. "This is a great job," she said, looking at Amelia who was jabbering and pointing skyward. "She's a happy little girl."

"Nate was crazy about her and I can see why." He made a funny face at the baby and she giggled at him.

"Much as I hate to leave, I've got to get back to work. Unless you need something," he said to Erin. "I'll see you both at dinner. Maisie will be in the house all afternoon and you can easily get in touch with me."

"We'll be fine. You go."

"Don't sound so eager," he said, smiling as he crossed the porch and held the door. "Are you two coming inside now?"

"Just long enough to get her stroller. I'll take her into the backyard. She seems to love being outside."

"Yes, she does. I know Nate would hold her in front of him on his horse."

"She's too little for that."

He held up his hands. "I'm not doing that yet. Right now I'm scared I'll drop her when I get her out of her bed."

Erin laughed. "Cade, you need to relax with her. You're not going to drop her when you pick her up."

"Everything I do with her I'm scared."

"That's too silly. Stop being so uptight."

"Stop laughing at me. I'm just an amateur dad," he said with a grin. "If you hadn't known me all your life, you wouldn't be laughing out loud at me and telling me I'm silly."

She had to admit he had a point there. She wiped away her grin and nodded at him. "You're doing great with her, Cade. We'll see you tonight."

When Cade went to his office, she looked down at Amelia as she strapped her in her stroller. "Your uncle Cade is scared to carry you, but he'll get over it soon," she cooed to the baby. "He's going to be a wonderful daddy for you, and he'll try to do everything your daddy would have done for you. And you'll love him because of it. In the meantime, I have to try to avoid falling in love with him." She pushed the stroller outside, all the time watching Cade walking toward the barns and garages.

Amelia began to babble and Erin nodded. "That's right." She laughed softly, thinking about Cade. She saw him already as a good dad and when he got more accustomed to Amelia, she knew he'd be a wonderful dad. She had a wistful pang and realized that his devotion to Amelia added to her attraction to him. It was one more strong pull on her heart, reinforcing an attraction that she was already fighting. An attraction that seemed to grow stronger every hour she was with him.

After Amelia's nap, Erin took her outside again. She was sitting in the shade on a lawn chair, Amelia in her stroller and gazing around, happy to be outside, when a bright red pickup pulled up by the back gate. The pickup had mud spattered on the tires and front bumper.

The door opened and a man—tall, broad-shouldered, wearing jeans, a Western shirt and wide-brimmed hat—jumped down. He opened the gate and stepped through, closing it and turning to come toward her.

"Hi. You must be Erin Dorsey. I'm Gabe Callahan, Cade's youngest brother," he said.

"I'm glad to meet you, Gabe."

"We may have met sometime way back in the past

when your brother was over or I was with Blake to pick up Cade, but I'm sure you don't remember it and I don't, either. Now though, I couldn't possibly forget meeting you." He smiled at her, his grin lighting up his handsome face. "I had no idea Luke had a gorgeous younger sister. Neither Luke nor Cade told me."

She laughed. "I doubt that is how your older brother would have described me. As a matter of fact, I seriously doubt if he ever described me at all." She shrugged. "When I was a kid, I don't think he even saw me. He never acknowledged me when we were in the same room together."

"Like I said, I'm sure that's changed now." Gabe grinned, another irresistible smile, revealing white, even teeth. Then he hunkered down in front of Amelia.

"Hi, baby," he said. "How's my favorite niece?" She blew bubbles in his direction and he chuckled. "You're a cutie."

He stood and turned back to Erin. She motioned to another lawn chair. "Pull a chair over and join us."

He sat in the grass, instead, facing both of them. "This will do. I won't be here long. I really won't if Cade catches me."

"Now, why is that? Why wouldn't your brother want you here?"

"Because he won't want me to come over and flirt with his nanny or ask his nanny to go dancing."

She had to smile as she shook her head. "I'd say you don't waste time, do you?"

He grinned, another infectious grin that made Amelia laugh.

"She likes your smile."

"The ladies often do," he said, leaning forward to look at Amelia. "You have excellent taste and a beautiful nanny, so I'll come see you often."

Amelia patted his cheek and he leaned out of her reach.

"Smart move," Erin remarked. "That little hand might be sticky."

"Do you like your job?" Gabe asked.

"I love taking care of her," she answered.

"Good. I know Cade is relieved. Actually all of us are because he needs a good nanny. He knows nothing about taking care of a baby. Same with me and the same with Blake, although Blake is going to become a dad in January and then he'll know a lot. Until then, we're three guys who haven't been around babies. Now, we can help with other things."

She smiled. "Right now, we're getting along pretty well."

"I asked and was told that you're a city woman, so I figure you like to get out and about. Cade said you have weekends free. Let me take you to eat scrumptious fried catfish and do some fun boot-scootin' this Saturday night."

She smiled at him again as she shook her head. "Thank you very much, but I can't do that. I told your brother that I'll work the next couple of weekends because he's unsure about taking care of Amelia all by himself."

"Okay, we'll make it the first weekend you're off work, then. You surely didn't agree to do that all the time?"

"No, I didn't. I'll have weekends free, but I'm not dating right now."

His gaze raked her from head to toe. "A pretty young thing like yourself?"

Erin suddenly remembered her brother's warning about Gabe Callahan. A ladies' man, a flirt. Well, once again her big brother was right.

Still, the man was trying to be nice, so she'd give him the courtesy of a reason. "I had a broken engagement recently."

He got up, picked up a lawn chair and placed it very close beside hers, turned slightly so he could face her.

"To my way of thinking, that breakup is the best reason to go out. It's a fun evening, no strings, just dancing and eating and meeting fun people and forgetting everything else. If you give me a chance, I'll bet I can make you forget all about that breakup for a little while on a Saturday night."

She had to smile. "I think the Callahans are born filled with confidence. You're very convincing, Gabe, but my answer is still the same. I'm not ready for an evening out with an energetic, enthusiastic, good-looking rancher."

Gabe was a fun, sexy cowboy who wanted to take her out. He seemed sweet and genuine and kind, and probably every female in the county would jump at the chance to go out with him. But not her. She felt not one arc of sizzling attraction to him. The kind of attraction that blazed between her and his brother.

Why did Cade have that effect on her?

Before she could dwell on that thought, Gabe let out a laugh. Then he leaned in closer, assessing her with his eyes. "I think you may be a challenge, Erin. I hate to see you stuck out here with my brother, who will be wringing his hands over what he needs to do for the little one and he won't even think of asking you to go dancing. Don't you know physical activity is one of the best ways to deal with stress?"

"Yes, I do and your brother has a gym in his house and a pool and I can use them daily."

"I might have to ask him if I can swim over here."

She smiled at him. "I'll tell you what you should do," she said, leaning forward slightly herself. "You find one of those pretty Texas women who love to party and dance and ask her out for Saturday night and go have a blast because she'll love it and you'll have fun."

"That's exactly what I'm trying to do, because I can't imagine that back before your breakup you weren't one of those pretty Texas women who liked to get out and enjoy life."

"It's not going to happen, cowboy. I'm not dating right now, but I do appreciate your invitation and your enthusiasm. Now, if you'd like to visit one night with your brother and Amelia and me, I think you'll find that she is adorable company."

"I'll take you up on that one on some weeknight because she is a cutie, and I've been over and played with her." He leaned back in his chair and crossed one booted foot over his knee. "You know, I told my brother that I was coming over to meet you and I was going to ask you out and he told me to go right ahead. He said you weren't dating and I would get turned down because you turn everyone down, so I know it wasn't just me, which is a good thing to learn."

"No, it's definitely not just you. Far from it. It's more just me right now."

"Well, I'll try again sometime, so you'll have another chance for a night out with me," he said, laughter dancing in his vivid blue eyes, and she had to smile again.

He stood and walked around to Amelia. "She's happy sitting there, so would you rather I didn't pick her up?"

"No, go ahead. She'll like the change and I'm surprised she's been content where she is this long."

He leaned down to get Amelia, unbuckled her and picked her up. "Hello, Amelia," he said while she tried to grab his hat.

Talking quietly to her, he walked away with her. "Want to look at the yard and the fence and my pretty red truck?"

Erin watched him walk around and show things to Amelia, who seemed happy with him, and she wondered again at the lack of physical response she had to an outright flirting and very good-looking young cowboy. Especially when a single glance from his brother would set her heart racing. What was it about Cade and the chemistry between them?

Gabe spent a long time walking and entertaining Amelia before he finally returned to strap her into her stroller again.

"There she is." He sat back down in the lawn chair and for the next twenty minutes they talked about grad school and life in general. Finally Amelia began to fuss and Erin stood up to take the stroller.

"I think it's nap time so unfortunately, Gabe, we'll have to tell you goodbye."

He stood. "It's been fun to meet you, Erin. I'll be back another time."

"It was interesting to meet you. Thanks again," she said. "You're good with Amelia."

"She's a little doll." He waved to Amelia. "Bye-bye, Amelia," he said as he turned to walk back to his truck. As Erin reached the door to go in, she saw his red truck disappear down the road.

While Amelia napped, Erin got some more of her things put away and when the baby stirred an hour later, Erin got a bath ready. She bathed Amelia, washing her thin, soft curls and later dressing her in a pale blue jumper and matching short-sleeved knit shirt.

They stayed in the playroom, Erin entertaining the baby by holding a big furry bear in front of her face and popping out to say "Peekaboo."

The first time she did it Amelia laughed. Delighted by the new sound of her laughter, Erin giggled in turn and repeated it, saying "Peekaboo" in a funny voice and getting more laughter.

She couldn't resist the third and fourth times. Amelia looked so adorable. When she heard a noise behind her, she turned to see Cade standing in the doorway. He was dusty and had a smudge of dirt on his jaw. His hair was tangled as he stood there watching her. And once again she felt that electric charge zing through her.

"I've never heard Amelia laugh like that," he said.

"Neither had I. Listen." She repeated the game, popping out from behind the bear, and Amelia gave another hearty laugh that made both Erin and Cade laugh in turn.

"I'll be damned," Cade said, entering the room. "I'm too dusty to pick her up," he said, waving his hand at himself while still watching his little niece.

Erin repeated her game and got another laugh. As she laughed she looked at Cade. "Adults will do anything to get a laugh from a little one. It's the most delightful sight and sound ever."

He studied Erin and she realized the cool remoteness he usually exhibited was gone. "You're great with her."

"I'm just playing with her," she said, but she was lost in his blue-eyed gaze that at the same time immobilized her and rocked her, no doubt from the sparks that flew between them. She knew he felt them, too.

Her pulse raced and then she realized how they were looking at each other, as if neither of them had seen the other before. As much as she wished she could sit there and feel his eyes on her all day, Amelia stirred and she turned to hand the child a rag doll. Then she picked Amelia up and placed her in her lap as she sat cross-legged on the blanket. All the time she felt as if Cade's gaze was still locked on her. When she finally glanced at him, she saw that she had been correct. He stood there watching her, his eyes like lasers trained on her and her alone.

She felt slightly uncomfortable, and searched for conversation. "Your brother came by today." It was the first thing that came to her.

"Gabe? He told me he would. Let me guess—he asked you out and you turned him down."

"You're right. He was fun and cheerful and very nice. I hope I didn't hurt his feelings."

"I don't think you did. Although he never gets turned down, so it's a new experience for him. He's even less serious with his women friends than I am."

The words came out before she could stop them. "Are these negative feelings about commitment all because of your dad? Your brother Nate married and so has your half brother, Blake."

"That they did. Nate never had negative feelings about marriage, though. I'm a year older and I hated the fights our parents had. Dad cut Blake out of his life and Dad went from wife to wife with mistresses in between—he spread a lot of misery. You have a wonderful family, so be thankful. I don't want to marry and risk that kind of upheaval ever. As far as my brother—I don't think Gabe is avoiding any serious relationship because of our dad. I just don't think Gabe's ready to settle down. He came close once when he was in college and none of us know much about her, but they dated a whole year, which is amazing for Gabe. Then she moved on and that was that. I've never heard of her since." He shrugged. "As far as asking you out, he'll be back."

"That's what he said."

As much as she wouldn't mind another invitation, it wasn't Gabe she pictured asking her out for a Saturday night on the town. It was this cowboy right in front of her.

Startled by the mental picture her errant thoughts conjured up, she turned her attention back to Amelia, and shifted her in her arms.

Cade must have sensed an end to the conversation, because he backed up. "I'll go get cleaned up so I can come back and hold her for a while," he said quietly, and then he turned and was gone.

When she heard his boots scrape the floor in the hall she finally let out her breath she didn't realize she was holding. So much for hoping this job would be easy and Cade would continue to be cool, remote and professional. He might remain professional, but it was already too late for cool and remote. That wall he'd had up the first day had vanished and she didn't think it would return.

Maybe he would surprise her and come back his quiet self—her employer who was polite, nice and remote. Not the tall handsome rancher who could make her heart pound with a glance and cause the temperature in the room to climb when he spoke to her. How was she going to resist that man through the coming months?

Far more immediate, how was she going to resist

him tonight when, after putting Amelia to bed, it was just the two of them in the house?

Cade spent the next two days getting up before sunrise and leaving, going out to work. On a ranch there was always work to do, and he was never so grateful for it. He intended to avoid the house—actually, he wanted to avoid Erin—as much as he could until evening when he wanted to spend time with Amelia.

He needed to get to know his niece and learn how to take care of her. From what he could see Erin was a marvelous nanny, as Luke had promised. Amelia liked her and every time he saw them together Amelia was happy. In the evening when Erin would play with her, he joined them. That was the most difficult part of his day. That was the time he couldn't avoid her anymore.

Flirting with Erin was a huge temptation. The more he tried to avoid her, the deeper his reaction was to her when they were together. She was a wonderful nanny and there was no way he could regret hiring her, but this was turning out to be a situation that left him sleepless at night.

Friday morning he changed his routine and lingered in the kitchen eating breakfast, thankful for Maisie's presence which helped him keep focused. Erin came through the door with Amelia in her arms. Erin's jeans were snug and a red knit shirt clung to a figure that made his pulse beat faster. Maisie was off on weekends, so they'd be alone after today. How was he going to ignore Erin all weekend, yet try to be with Amelia? Just the thought made his throat dry up.

"Good morning," Erin said, looking wide-eyed at him. "I'm surprised to see you here."

Amelia held out her arms to Cade. Startled, he stood to take her. "Good morning and hello to you, Amelia," he said. He looked back at Erin. "That's the first time she's made it obvious she wanted to come to me."

Erin smiled at him. "That's good. She'll do it more. You'll see. Can you stay and hold her for a few minutes? It'll be good for both of you to be together."

"Sure," he said, looking at Amelia as she ran her small hand over his jaw.

"There's our pretty girl," Maisie said, bringing a bowl of fluffy yellow scrambled eggs to the table. "Aren't you the cute one," she cooed softly to Amelia. The baby smiled and reached out for Maisie, making all the adults laugh.

"So much for her wanting to be with me," Cade remarked.

Maisie reached for her. "I'll take her. I'm through cooking now anyway." She took Amelia, who nestled against her as she walked away to the window. The cook talked softly to Amelia, trying to get her to look outside. "I'll take her out for a few minutes so you two can have breakfast in peace," Maisie said. "She likes to look around and then she can eat."

"Sure," Cade answered at the same time Erin said to go ahead. They looked at each other and laughed. "I'll try to let you field the questions about Amelia," he said as Maisie stepped outside with the baby and closed the door behind her, leaving them alone in the kitchen.

He held a chair at the table for Erin near Amelia's high chair. "Ready for breakfast?"

"Yes, thanks," she answered politely, taking a seat. As she did, he caught the faintest sweet scent, which could have been from baby powder, from perfume or from an early-morning shower. Instead of lingering on the scent, he tried to focus on breakfast, sitting down and passing the bowl of scrambled eggs to Erin.

"Thank you," she said without looking at him, keeping her attention on the bowl of eggs as she took it from him. Her fingers brushed his and she drew a deep breath.

"Maisie better get the hell back in here before I say something I shouldn't," Cade said, and Erin glanced up with a wide-eyed, startled look.

"I think you're right," she whispered, confirming his assumption that she had as much a reaction to him as he had to her.

"I hate to step out there and get her to come in because she'll think we don't want her to carry Amelia around, which is not the case. I'll be right back," he said, leaving the room. He forced himself to think about Luke and remember his best friend telling him that he felt certain he could count on Cade to be professional around his sister, telling him how vulnerable she was. It was a litany he chanted more and more often. Not that it seemed to be doing much good. He walked down the hall with clenched fists. He wanted her in his arms and he wanted to kiss her. To be truthful, he wanted to seduce her, make love to her. But he wouldn't—couldn't—cross that line. He couldn't allow himself to be the cause of any more hurt. And if he knew one thing about Erin, he knew she was way too earnest to take seduction lightly.

"Damn," he said quietly, feeling caught in a dilemma. It was August—how was he going to cope with being with her every day until mid-December?

He would be gone some because of business and during the day he was out working, but he wanted to bond with Amelia and the only way to do that was to spend time with her—time he'd also be spending with Erin. What was he to do?

He had reached the front door and stood looking through the sidelights flanking the wide, oversize door. He stared at his front porch and yard without seeing, either. In his mind's eye all he saw were Erin's big green eyes, her long legs, her tempting curves and ready smile.

"Where the hell is your willpower, Callahan?" he asked himself softly. But he couldn't answer his own question. He thought maybe the best thing would be to hear Luke's voice. More than anything he wanted to call his friend, but he was probably already out of touch. No, Cade was on his own here.

Taking a deep breath and determined to resist Erin and remain professional, he headed back to the kitchen. To his relief Maisie had returned, Amelia was buckled into her chair and Erin was giving her tiny bites of cut-up banana that she could pick up and feed herself. Erin talked softly to her as she placed a little cup with a lid in front of Amelia.

He figured he'd give it a shot. "Erin, do you know if I can get through to your brother?" When she looked at him questioningly, he bluffed. "I thought you might like to talk to him."

Her taut look eased. "He sends me texts. A phone call will be expensive. Right now he's in São Paulo, Brazil, for a few more days and then he continues on south." She glanced at the kitchen clock. "If you want to get in touch with him, the time is fine now. It's around noontime there."

"Great. Let's call him after breakfast." Cade resumed his seat and tried to keep his attention on his plate, Amelia, Maisie—everything around him except Erin—but he failed. His gaze swept over her, taking in each and every curve that her knit shirt revealed. Was he the only one who felt as if the temperature in the kitchen had climbed to uncomfortable heights? Finally, he stood, cutting short his breakfast, knowing he had to get out of the house before he did something foolish. Like flirt or ask her out.

He stepped into the hall, walked to his office, allowing himself to cool down. When nothing worked he called Luke and blew out a breath when he finally heard him answer. "Good morning. Or afternoon. It's Cade…No, everything's fine," he reassured his friend when he expressed concern. "I just thought we'd call you. Here's Erin." He walked back into the kitchen and handed her the phone, turning his attention to helping Amelia who was doing quite well on her own and sipping from her small sippy cup.

The reception had been fair when he'd told Luke hello and since Erin was speaking more loudly than normal, he assumed the reception was poor, but then her voice dropped back to the usual conversational level as she talked about Amelia and being on the ranch and the weather. He listened as she asked Luke what he was doing and finally, she looked at Cade.

"I'll let Cade say hello. This call was his idea and we're talking on his phone," she said, listened a moment and laughed as she handed the phone to Cade.

"Hi, buddy," Cade said. "I thought we'd see if you're frozen yet, but instead you're partying it up in Brazil."

"Long, tedious meetings that end tomorrow, thank goodness. Food is great here and the nights are fun, as a matter of fact." He paused a second, then said, "I know I don't have to ask you to know Erin is doing a good job."

"Absolutely. She's a marvelous nanny," he said, meeting Erin's green-eyed gaze and seeing her mouth form a "thank you."

"She has bonded with Amelia and I'm slowly, very slowly, learning how to deal with Amelia."

"Yeah." Luke's voice came clearly enough that Cade recognized the sarcasm in his tone. "I know why you called. You're having a difficult time trying to keep from flirting with her. Remember, she's vulnerable," he said slowly and clearly. "She's been hurt badly."

"I'm very aware of that," Cade said cheerfully, hoping Erin didn't guess the drift of the call.

"I know she can take care of herself, but you have a way with the ladies, so keep in mind that she's my sister, that she is hurting and she doesn't need to hurt even more."

"Sure thing. You keep from freezing if you ever leave São Paulo."

"I will and you remember what I've told you. I don't know if I can get through from where I'll be, so I'm glad you called and let me talk to her. She sounds happy, which means she likes being with Amelia and I think it's good for her to have to take care of your little girl."

"I hope so. Amelia's certainly happy over it. I'll give the phone back to Erin. Good talking to you." He wanted to add, "I think," but he didn't. He handed the phone to Erin carefully, making sure their hands didn't touch.

He stood and walked away from her, thinking about her brother, trying to focus on Luke, to think about Erin's broken engagement, her canceled wedding, her miscarriage. He vowed to himself that he would exercise self-control, willpower, and resist the attraction that seemed to increase by the hour.

It had helped to talk with Luke. He should be able to keep his promises to Luke, control his feelings and longings and remain professional. Erin obviously was fighting the same battle to some extent, but he didn't think she felt the attraction to the depth and intensity that he did. If she did…

Realizing where his thoughts were leading, he

tried to focus on the ranch and the roof that needed to be checked after the last hailstorm.

He wanted to go to Fort Worth to a cattle sale and pick up a new bull.

"If you need me, call," he said, leaning down to brush a quick kiss on Amelia's cheek and getting a sticky hand on his cheek that made him laugh.

"Thanks, Amelia," he said, going to the sink to wash his cheek, then grabbing a paper towel to dry it, while Erin told her brother goodbye and ended the call.

"Do you see any food on my face?" He had intended to ask Maisie, but she had moved away and Erin stood nearby, so she stepped close to look at his face.

He inhaled and caught the faint sweet scent again. Her skin was smooth, flawless and her cheeks rosy. Her lips were full, heart-shaped, tempting. He was caught and held as he looked into her green eyes. "Anything on my face?" he repeated in a husky voice.

Her gaze moved slowly over him and his pulse raced so fast he could barely get his breath. He should turn and get out of the kitchen, but for some reason he couldn't seem to move.

She focused on his cheek and took the paper towel from him to dab at his face. "There. Now there's not," she said softly and met his gaze.

"Thanks," he whispered. He finally got his legs to obey his silent command and left the kitchen as if he was being chased. Outside in the cool morning air, he wiped his suddenly sweaty brow and let out his breath.

He had one humdinger of a dilemma on his hands.

He didn't want to stay away from Amelia. This was a critical time when she was adjusting to him, to new people and a new home. He needed to be there for her, but Erin was one of the most appealing women he had ever met. And he needed to steer clear of her. So what could he do? He stood outside, staring across the yard, lost in thought and not even knowing where he was.

Why did Luke's sister have to be this red-hot alluring woman who took his breath away, made his heart pound and muddled his thinking? Of all the women he had ever known, Erin Dorsey was the one woman he should not have any interest in other than as a nanny. She was far too vulnerable. She wasn't his type. And she was his employee. Most of all, she was his lifelong best friend's sister and if he hurt her, he would lose the best friend he had ever had.

As he headed to the garage to get his pickup, he realized Erin had probably gotten the same warnings from Luke to resist her boss and clear reminders how Cade would never be serious about a woman or have a real relationship with any meaning.

He hoped Luke had warned her. He had been on the verge of it himself.

He realized he was standing by his pickup, lost in thought about Erin. She was distracting. Maybe if he kissed her once, he would be satisfied and then leave her alone.

"Yeah, right," he said as he climbed into his truck and pulled out.

* * *

Erin had changed for dinner while Amelia napped, into a dark green, sleeveless, cotton sundress with a full skirt that was not too short, not too revealing. Just right for dinner with Amelia and Cade.

After Amelia's nap Erin changed her into a pretty new jumper and took her outside in the shady yard to take some pictures. Over the last few days she'd noticed that Cade had no photos of the baby anywhere in the house.

"You don't want to grow up without pictures, do you?" she asked Amelia. Despite knowing she wouldn't get an answer, she talked constantly to Amelia anyway, because that was how babies came to learn.

She took a couple of shots with her phone, then sent several to her parents and two to Luke. Since he was a bachelor, she didn't know how much he would be interested in Amelia's pictures, but she thought Amelia looked so cute, she didn't know how anyone could keep from enjoying seeing her pictures. Then she sent several to Cade so he'd have some on his phone as well as in his house.

Just thinking about him made her pulse quicken. In a few hours, when he returned and Maisie left for the evening, they'd be alone. With Amelia, of course. Until she went to bed. And then…? Every inch of her tingled as she let herself fantasize about what kind of night they'd have. Alone with a sexy man who had such a sensual effect on her—

No! She pushed those thoughts out of her mind, refusing to indulge those enticing images. What was she thinking? Cade Callahan may be a handsome rancher but he was her boss. And tonight was nothing more than work. Caring for her charge and sharing a meal with her employer.

That was all it could be.

She heard the gate open behind her and turned toward it. When she took in the sight, her breath caught in her throat. In a wide-brimmed black hat, tight jeans, boots and a fitted, blue cotton shirt that reflected his eyes, Cade strode toward her, his gaze never leaving hers.

And right then and there she knew she was in big trouble.

Four

Cade crossed the yard to them, his long legs eating up the distance. "Hi. What's happening?" he asked, his gaze going over her, making her aware of her sundress and the breeze tugging at her hair. She held down her skirt.

"We're out for a stroll," she replied, not liking the deep tone to her voice. She wanted to clear her throat but didn't want to be too obvious. "Amelia likes to be outside."

"It's cooling off some now and I suppose it's comfy in the shade, especially if you're not tossing trimmed brush into a truck bed." He dusted off his jeans and hunkered down in front of Amelia in her stroller.

"Hi, little doll," he said, smiling at Amelia who babbled and grabbed the brim of his hat, tugging lightly, but not able to pull it off. He pushed it back on his head. "Thanks for her pictures," he said without turning to look at Erin.

"You're welcome. You should have pictures of her on your phone to show people. And we should print some out and frame them for the house. I'll do that. Also, Cade, I think she'd like a swing out here. You have some big tree limbs that are low enough. She loves being outside and she likes her inside swing so…"

He stood to face Erin and her heartbeat quickened as she looked up at him. She rolled the stroller slightly back and forth to entertain Amelia. As Cade glanced around, her gaze ran over his jaw that now had a faint shadow from the stubble of his beard. His clothes and boots were dusty and he had a smudge on his cheek. Just the sight of him made her tingle from head to toe. Her body nearly cried out with longing, making it hard to hear the echo of her brother's reminders and warnings on the phone earlier. Luke had told her again that Cade would never be serious about a relationship. He'd repeated that Cade was a die-hard bachelor and intended to stay that way all his life. He was deeply opposed to marriage.

The words reverberated in her head till he smiled, and then she didn't hear a one of them.

"You're right," Cade said. "I don't know why I didn't think of a swing for her." He looked up at the tree they stood under, searching for the perfect limb. "I guess I was so busy trying to figure out what I needed to do to care for her each day, a swing never entered—"

He broke off as he turned to look at her and his eyes narrowed. He drew a deep breath and she felt her cheeks flush with heat. Suddenly self-conscious, she bent down to smooth Amelia's collar that didn't need smoothing. She didn't know what Cade had seen in her expression, but he must have guessed her thoughts were personal and on him.

"You look pretty," he said in a husky voice.

She was grateful she wasn't looking at him or he would have seen the desire that flared to life in her eyes. She busied herself with fidgeting with Amelia's jumper, which probably lasted only a couple of seconds but felt like an eternity. By the time she straightened, he was backing up, his hat in his hand.

"I'll go clean up and see you at dinner," he said abruptly and turned to stride toward the house, his long legs covering the ground swiftly.

She felt bereft at his departure. But she knew why he'd left so suddenly. His tone of voice had been thick and deep. There was no denying the fiery attraction he'd felt. She had felt it, too. And there was no way she'd be able to resist him if he ever broke down that wall of self-control he'd erected around himself.

If that happened, she'd be tumbling headfirst into heartbreak.

Taking a deep breath, she pushed the stroller back to the house and stepped into the much-needed air-conditioning just as Maisie was leaving.

"Dinner is ready. I told Cade and he left to clean up. Can I do anything else before I go?"

"No, thank you, Maisie. Thanks so much for all you did today."

"I'll see you Monday morning unless you need me before then."

"Thanks. Have a nice weekend," Erin said. But what she really wanted to say was that they needed her to stay for the weekend and be a third person with them. But that was wishful thinking.

She remembered from her interview that Cade had asked for her to stay with Amelia on Friday evenings so he could go out and she wished he was starting tonight, but he hadn't said a word about going any-where away from the ranch. She'd better get a grip because it was going to be a long night.

She got Amelia out of her stroller and took her to the sitting room where she spread out a blanket and sat down to play with her. She was playing patty-cake as Cade came into the room and for an instant she forgot what she was doing when she glanced at him. He had showered and changed. He still had a faint stubble of beard, but his hair was combed with waves already curling on his forehead, the ends still damp from his shower. He wore a blue dress shirt open at the throat and tucked into fresh jeans with a different pair of clean, black hand-tooled boots and a leather belt around his narrow waist.

"Come join us."

"How about a glass of wine? Or a beer?"

"I'll take white wine, thank you. Would you please

bring her sippy cup with some water in case she gets thirsty?"

He nodded and returned with the white wine, a bottle of cold beer and a cup that he handed to Amelia. He joined them on the floor.

She latched on to a safe topic. "You asked me to stay these few weekends, so if it's all right with you, tomorrow you can help with Amelia and learn how to take care of her all on your own."

"That still scares the hell out of me. I don't know what to do, but I'm watching to see what you and Maisie do. My grandmother was almost as much at a loss as I am."

"She was sweet to stay until you got a nanny."

"You're a great nanny and I'm so thankful you took the job."

"Which brings up something I want to talk to you about."

His blue eyes focused on her and he arched a dark eyebrow in question.

"Amelia is babbling and imitating sounds. I'd like to start using words around her so she can begin to learn them. Is she going to call you daddy or Uncle Cade?" As he started to answer, she held her hand up. "Think a minute. You will raise her and you will be a dad to her."

"I'm never taking Nate's place," Cade said, frowning. "Nate was her dad and is forever her dad."

"Of course. I know that and she will, too, when she is slightly older and can understand, but in practical everyday living, you're going to be Dad to her. If this were reversed would you want your child calling your brother Uncle or Dad? She'll know Nate was her daddy because you'll see to that and have his pictures around, but in a lot of ways, you're going to have to be her dad and you need to decide what she'll call you."

Cade looked away and a muscle worked in his jaw. "Sometimes that wreck hits me. I miss Nate. I miss Nate and Lydia having their baby."

"I know you do," Erin said quietly, giving him a moment to deal with his emotions.

Finally he took a deep breath and faced her again. "Amelia isn't talking yet and I haven't given that a thought. Let me sleep on it."

"You do that, but let me know because before long, this little girl is going to be saying simple words and I can teach her something to call you before I go." She smiled. "Uncle Cade is a mouthful, I have to say, and will probably come out like *Unca Kay.* Or maybe she'll just call you *Okay.* That's an incentive to make a decision." He grinned and she smiled deeper, unable to resist his grin. When she put Amelia to bed tonight, she had to go to her room and get away from him, no matter how tempting it was to come back to talk to him.

"Will you entertain her while I put our dinner on the table and we can eat?" Erin said. "It smells wonderful, some kind of enchilada casserole."

"Sounds good to me," he said. "What's our baby having? More mashed stuff that bears little resemblance to real food?"

"Something healthy, pureed for babies."

"Good thing you didn't leave me to feed her to-night," he said, making a silly noise and causing Amelia to laugh.

As Erin got dinner on the table, she watched Cade playing with Amelia. For a man who didn't want to ever marry, he was such a good daddy. He seemed to be having as much fun playing as Amelia was having. Impulsively, Erin took their picture, both of them laughing while Cade held Amelia in the crook of his arm and made silly noises and faces. Erin couldn't keep from laughing at them—until she was struck by the power of the moment. It was one of those times when she was knocked over by the realization of her own loss and she felt a sharp stab of pain right to her heart.

Turning away from them, she hurried to get dinner on the table.

Later, after they'd finished, when she finally stood and told Cade she was taking Amelia to bed, she stopped in the doorway. "I won't come back tonight. I'll see you in the morning."

"I know you're not going to sleep this early. Come back and talk for a while. I'll stay clear over here on my side of the room and you can stay way over there and we won't cross the middle of the room. How safe is that?"

She stared at him in surprise that he had openly acknowledged they were trying to avoid each other. He hadn't admitted why, but they both knew why. "It might be safe, might not, but it's not very smart," she answered with a breathlessness that she couldn't avoid.

"Live dangerously, Erin. Your brother has warned you so much about me that I'm sure you'll do what he told you. He's threatened to punch me out if I do anything I shouldn't and I don't particularly want that, nor do I want to lose his friendship which goes way back in our young lives. So come back and let's sit and talk and keep our distance and all will be well. Otherwise, I might have to come get you and try to talk you into coming back here with me. That would throw us much closer together."

"You're a bit devious, aren't you?" she said, smiling and knowing she couldn't say no. "I'll be back."

"That's good," he said as she walked away.

At the door she turned. "It'll be a while. I rock her and read at least one or two stories to her. Don't look for me soon and don't come to get me because I'm not leaving her until she's down for the night."

"I wouldn't think of taking you away from rocking her or reading to her. I think that's wonderful. I'd love it if you—"

"Shh," she said, stopping him from voicing what she thought was coming. "Whatever you're about to say, don't say it. We're doing pretty well keeping things impersonal. Pretty well. I'd say maybe good enough to rate a C+. Don't pull down that grade."

"C+? I think I deserve an A."

"Don't push your luck," she said, turning to leave because they were verging on losing that professionalism they each had been struggling to demonstrate.

She didn't look back as she left, carrying Amelia to get her ready for bed. Erin no longer wondered how she would get through the weekend with him. Instead, she fretted over how she would get through the next few hours.

She needed to continue the remote, polite, professional relationship of a rancher and his nanny.

Would that even be possible? Why was she so drawn to him? She had been hurt, and numb around all other men since her broken engagement. What was it about Cade that had been instant, intense and an irresistible attraction even when she knew she should never become emotionally involved with him?

Could she spend the next few hours with him without ending up in his arms and without kissing him?

Cade went outside and stood on the back porch, looking at the yard. He had yard lights and lights in the trees so it was easy to see close to the porch, and he looked again at tree limbs where he could hang a swing. He was losing his fear of carrying Amelia, of holding her too tightly, of scaring her with his deep voice. He no longer had to worry about what to feed her because Erin and Maisie both knew. Erin would be present when Maisie went home.

Now his worries shifted to Erin. His call to Luke brought back all the warnings, the emphasis on the heartaches she had just been through, the threats by Luke to end their friendship if Cade hurt her.

Cade knew exactly what he should do, but he was more drawn to her by the hour and he couldn't explain why, except she was sexy, gorgeous, fun and intelligent. That was a deadly combination when he was living under the same roof with her. It made him want to get to know the appealing woman she was. Get to know her and get her into his bed. But he could not do any such thing because too much was at stake—his lifelong friendship with his best friend and her fragile peace of mind after going through two heartbreaks.

No, he needed to fortify that wall around himself so he could stay on the ranch with Erin and learn how to take care of Amelia. But how in sweet hell would he survive night after night of putting Amelia to bed early and then staying alone with her nanny? Amelia's gorgeous, sexy nanny that he wanted to seduce?

"Dammit."

He went upstairs quietly because he had learned one thing—don't wake a baby that is dozing off. He had learned long ago how to move without making noise, so he tiptoed to open his connecting door.

As he looked into Amelia's room, he stood riveted. Erin held her close in her arms, rocking her. A small lamp burned with only low light in the room, but Cade could see the tears running down Erin's cheeks.

The lamp caught highlights in her red-gold hair that spilled over her shoulders. Taken aback because she was hurting, he closed the door quietly and walked away.

He wanted to cross the room and hold her and comfort her, but he didn't dare. Sympathy would turn to desire as quickly as a lightning bolt streaking across the sky.

He stood thinking about her and wondered whether she was crying over the baby she lost or the guy she lost or both. Was she still in love with him? The guy couldn't have really been in love and dumped her the way he did.

Cade thought of his dad and the three women he had married and the mistresses and the misery he had caused. Once again he promised himself that he would never get married. Returning to the sitting area, he picked up toys and put away the blanket. Then he cleaned the kitchen and was finishing when he turned to find Erin standing in the doorway.

"I was gone the right amount of time," she said, joking with him when she entered the room, and if he hadn't seen the tears on her cheeks, he wouldn't have guessed she had had a bad minute since she'd left him to put Amelia down.

"Ready for some relaxation—more wine, play a game, watch something or just sit?" he asked.

"I vote for just sit. For a little person who doesn't talk yet, I seem to have a lot of conversation with her."

"I'm getting a beer. I didn't drink that first one, but it's no longer cold." He grabbed a bottle from the fridge. "Now let's go sit and you can take one side of the room and I'll take the other and if we're tempted to meet in the center, we can imagine your brother sitting in the middle of the room."

She laughed. "Luke values your friendship. You know he does."

"Not as much as he wants his baby sister to avoid

getting hurt. I don't blame him. I wasn't happy about my half brother getting hurt."

"How was that?"

"I figured you'd heard Luke say something because he knew. C'mon, let's sit and I'll tell you," Cade said, walking into the adjoining sitting area.

"Oh, my, you picked up all Amelia's toys and put them away. You're catching on to being a dad. Very good."

"I am very good," he said, flirting and not thinking about toys.

She blinked and her eyes sparkled. "Modest, too," she teased back at him. "Cleaned the kitchen, put away the toys. Very talented man," she said, turning swiftly to sit in a wing chair. The full skirt of her sundress swirled around her legs and flew up over her knees. She flipped her skirt down and crossed her long legs, looking up to see him looking at her legs. His gaze met hers.

"I'm talented in other areas, too," he drawled. "You'd be surprised."

She smiled at him. "I don't think I'll pursue what you're so talented at tonight. You were going to talk about your half brother. That should be a safe topic."

Cade crossed the room, sat in the big leather chair he liked, propped his feet on the matching ottoman and settled back, thinking he could look at her all night. The soft light picked up the blond highlights in her red hair that spilled over her shoulders. The top of her sundress revealed the beginnings of the lush curves of her creamy breasts. Her skin was perfect, smooth, ivory and so soft-looking.

He wanted to cross the room, pick her up and place her on his lap and kiss her. He thought about her upstairs, crying over her losses, rocking and holding Amelia, who had also had big losses.

He didn't want to add any more hurt to what Erin had already gone through, so he settled back in the chair and looked out the window at the lighted yard while he went back to a safer topic.

"My family history is not the best ever. When Dad divorced Veronica, Blake was too little to understand what was happening. Dad cut Veronica and Blake out of his life completely. I don't think Blake was a year old. As a child, Blake had no memory of his dad ever speaking to him."

"He was a tiny baby. How could a dad not speak to his own child?"

"Blake said his mother told him that it was because his dad was angry with her. Whatever the reason, he ignored Blake. Blake wasn't any part of our lives, either—we didn't know who he was when we were little, and then had nothing to do with him because that's what we were taught. Our mothers didn't get along."

"That might have been because of your dad, too."

"I don't know. Actually, we never saw a lot of our dad, but our relationships with him weren't as bad as the way he snubbed Blake. He didn't pay much attention to the three of us and we all went to military schools."

"Was he a solitary person?"

Cade smiled. "He was a wealthy person. He spent his energies making money and that's what he loved. Money and power. He's a multibillionaire. There were mistresses and Mom divorced him. When Mom and Dad divorced, we hardly saw him, but he would show up at a graduation or something big."

"I can't imagine a father being that way," she said, shaking her head. "I have such a good dad."

"Yes, you do. I know him and he's a good father. He's friendly and great with kids. Anyway, Blake and I are the same age and in high school we realized there wasn't any reason to dislike each other. We became close friends and I brought him into the family. He never came to anything if our dad was there until the past year. We can thank Sierra for causing Blake to lose a lot of his bitterness and to actually contact our dad and want to meet him. They have a truce of sorts now."

"Sierra must have been a good influence."

"She was, but it's too late. Our dad means nothing to Blake. Our Mom, Crystal, was around, but her big interest was her social life, so we had nannies. Just like you and Luke, we grew up in Downly. Your family stayed in Downly, mine acquired a Dallas home, too, which is where Mom still lives if she ever comes home. Our grandfather had a ranch—that's where we spent a lot of time. Some of that you should know from Luke."

"I didn't ask Luke about his friends' backgrounds."

"Well, now you have a chunk of my sordid family history."

"It's awful he cut his son out of his life. Blake was only a little baby," she said again.

"Relationships are important. I don't want to lose your brother's friendship. He's meant too much to me for too long. Besides, I wouldn't want to do one thing to hurt his little sister."

He received one of her high-voltage dimpled smiles and felt his insides clutch. "Now why would you possibly hurt me?" she asked.

"Never deliberately."

"There must be a 'bad-boy' side to you that worries Luke," she said in a throaty voice.

The room suddenly became too hot and she was sitting too far away. He wanted to reach for her and toss an answer back at her. Before he could, she suddenly looked startled as if she just realized the direction of their conversation and her smile vanished.

"Whoops. I forgot the situation for a moment there." She fanned herself. "You made me forget all about my brother, his warnings and all I've heard about you. I remembered in the nick of time. I think we'll go on to a new topic." She paused a moment, then settled on a safe question. "Is this a cattle ranch, horse ranch? I don't really know much about you even though you and Luke have known each other for a long time."

For a minute he didn't answer her. His head spun with her changes, but he had discovered that she could be sexy, could be fun, could flirt and she might like to kiss—knowledge that aroused him, made him hot, made him want her more. He struggled to follow her to the safe conversation, fighting his way back to the guardian/nanny roles.

"It's a cattle ranch," he finally replied, "but I have other interests. I work with Gabe in commercial real estate, but I'm easing away from that because of Amelia. I prefer the life of a rancher and since I can afford to do what I want, I can live here and work at what I like best."

"I suspect being a rancher involves some rough, hard and dangerous work—more than being in an office, although driving through traffic to get to work can be dangerous, very hazardous."

"There are challenges here, along with rewards, satisfaction for getting out and doing things that are physical. You want to work with children, which is good—you're great at it."

"I like child psychology. I like human services and counseling children. Actually, there are a lot of possibilities. I think I may be able to choose where I want to work. My brother, on the other hand, wants to be in the exotic spots, although an environmental engineer can work all over the world."

"He won't find any frozen tundra in Texas," he said, and she smiled.

As the evening passed, he found her easy to talk to which was no surprise because in some ways she was a little like her brother, plus they had grown up in the same general area and gone to the same schools, even though she was several years younger. He kept

on track, constantly thinking about Luke, but it took
an effort, especially when they laughed together over
a humorous episode in their pasts.

Her laughter was infectious and enticing and always stirred the desire to kiss her. Kissing her was
never far from his thoughts. Each time, he had to
think about Luke, remember seeing her rocking and
crying. He suspected from here on, he should find
something else to do with his evenings after one or
the other of them put Amelia to bed.

"You asked me about going out on Friday nights,"
she said at one point. "Please feel free to do so, Friday
or Saturday night. I don't mind staying and I won't
be going back to Dallas a lot of weekends, so I can
take care of Amelia."

"You're trying to get rid of me," he said, amused
that she was urging him to go somewhere.

"I might be," she said with that mischievous look
she'd had a couple of times when she relaxed about
being with him.

"Right now, there isn't anyone in particular I'm
seeing and nothing much going on, so it's okay to stay
home. I can say the same thing to you—the weekends
are yours, after this first month. This one I'd like to
stay at your side and see what you do to take care of
Amelia and what I should feed her."

"I'd be glad to," she agreed. "You've got nothing
to worry about. Amelia's a good baby. She's been
sleeping so well, which is great because some little
kids don't. She likes her food and she's happy most
of the time. She's a happy, easy baby so you're in luck

there." Erin stood and he came to his feet. "Sounds like we've got a busy day tomorrow, so I think I'll go to my room now. I'll see you in the morning. And remember, if you want to go out tomorrow night, go right ahead. I'll be here anyway."

Amused, he smiled because he was certain she was trying to get him out of the house. "I'll think about it. It would probably be better for both of us if I did something, even if it's just driving to Downly or points north, south, east or west and getting away from temptation."

As she nodded, her cheeks flushed. "I think that's an excellent idea. If you don't want to do that, maybe I will. It'll be a nice summer evening. "Good night, Cade," she said, and turned for the door.

Remaining where he was, he watched her leave without answering her. What he wanted to do was walk down the hall with her or try to talk her into staying longer because it wasn't late, but he knew better. As she left the room, he let out his breath.

He had to get out of the house tomorrow night because she had flat out asked him to do so or told him if he didn't, she would. He thought about women he usually liked to take out and quickly rejected each one. He'd go to dinner in Downly and find somewhere to go for a beer, spend some time and come home late.

He had a lot of nights and a lot of weekends ahead of him, so he better find something to do or someone else who interested him.

He stood with his hands on his hips. He was on edge. Maybe he should work out, he thought. But he didn't feel like going into his home gym. All he wanted was her back in the room so they could at least talk.

Finally he went to his room to change. He'd just pulled off his boots when he heard Amelia crying. He glanced at the closed door to her room and waited a moment, but as she continued crying, he crossed the room.

Her crying stopped and he wondered if she had gone back to sleep or if Erin was with her. He waited a moment and then knocked lightly on the door.

"Come in," Erin called, so he opened the door and entered to find Erin holding Amelia. The baby clung to Erin's shoulder, but turned when he entered to look at him.

"I heard her crying."

"Maybe she heard me say what a wonderful sleeper she is and decided she would prove me wrong," Erin said, smiling at Amelia. Amelia stared at Cade and held her tiny arms out, reaching for him.

"Hey, she wants to go to you. See, she likes for you to hold her," Erin said, crossing the room to hand Amelia to him.

He wanted to wrap his arms around both of them. Instead, he took Amelia who was warm, soft and smelled faintly of baby powder. "What's disturbing our baby?" he asked her softly, turning to walk with her. She wrapped her arm around his neck and clung to him, seeming to be happy as far as he could tell.

He should tell Erin to go on to bed, that he would rock Amelia back to sleep and put her in her crib, but he didn't want Erin to go. Still in her green sundress, she stood looking at him. In the soft light of one small lamp she looked more enticing than ever.

"I'd feel better if you'd stay," he said to Erin. "Do you mind?"

"Of course not," she answered, holding back a smile. "I wasn't going far away," she added, glancing at the open door to her suite.

"I know. I'll walk her a little and then rock her a little if she likes to rock."

"Fine, but give her to me whenever you want, although she looks very happy now with your arms around her. I don't know why she's awake."

"She'll go back to sleep," he said quietly walking around the room with her and then sitting in the rocker to rock her while Erin had already settled in a large, overstuffed chair.

After a few minutes Amelia placed her head on his shoulder.

"When her eyes close, tell me," he whispered.

"Her eyes are already closed. I think she'll go to sleep," Erin said softly.

Cade continued rocking for another twenty minutes while he talked quietly to Erin.

"She is definitely asleep," Erin told him.

"I'll put her in her bed now," he said, handling her with great care as he stood and placed her in her crib. Erin came to stand beside him.

"See, she's sound asleep."

"It's early, Erin. I'm not going to bite. Come back

and let's have cookies and milk or something and talk awhile longer."

Her green eyes widened as she gazed at him with a slight frown and didn't answer.

"I've kept my distance and haven't flirted. C'mon. It'll be more fun than sitting alone and I'm hours from sleep."

"Against all good judgment, I'll go with you for a while," she said. "It's early and Amelia seems sound asleep."

Satisfaction made him smile when she nodded and walked beside him. They paused at the door to both look back at Amelia, who was asleep curled on her side.

After he got some crackers, cheese, ice water for her and a cold beer for himself, they sat in the screened part of his porch on the darker east side of his house.

"I have fewer trees on this side of the house—the three oaks are it for now and they each have a couple of lights, but nothing like the other sides. I enjoy sitting out here in the dark sometimes. I can switch those lights off so it's dark enough to see some stars."

Their voices were soft in the quiet night. She had her iPad open, the brightness dimmed, but he could see Amelia hadn't moved since they left her.

He put his feet on another chair and talked quietly to Erin. "This is the most peaceful place on earth."

"You love it here, don't you?"

"Yes. I love everything about it except the paperwork. I can't totally escape that, what with keeping records, making sure taxes are right."

"Why don't you just do this all the time?"

"I wanted a business, to make money and not live on what Dad has given us. Just another little way to try to break away from him now that I'm grown."

"Cade, you're already becoming a good daddy for Amelia. You're not the same man as your dad, you know."

"Damn, I hope not. Are you going to give me a pitch on how great it would be to get married?"

She laughed softly, a tempting sound that made him want to draw her close. "It's just ridiculous for you to decide you'll never marry because your dad couldn't stay happily married. You're a different person."

"Amen. His blood is in my veins, though. I don't want any part of settling down."

"That's a shame," she said. "You're good with Amelia."

"I still feel nervous, but not as much as I did. Each day I feel closer to her. I hope she likes the ranch."

"She'll love it because it's her home."

"I suppose you're right there. Think you'll look for work in this area after you get your degree?"

"I'll look, but I'll go where the job is."

"That's good. If you end up somewhere else, will you come back and see us?"

"I can't answer that one now. Amelia may not even remember me because she's so young."

"I'll remember you," he said and she laughed.

"I'd hope. You've known me forever."

The later they talked, the longer they were together, the more he wanted to hold her and kiss her.

She finally stood and the last time he had looked at his watch, it had been after one in the morning. He guessed it might be after two. When she reached to pick up her glass and plate, he stood, his fingers closing around her wrist lightly.

"You don't—" Cade had started to tell her she didn't need to carry her dishes to the kitchen. The minute he took her slender wrist, the words vanished.

He drew a deep breath while a tingling current sizzled and sent his temperature soaring. He had made a tactical mistake, a monumental blunder in his effort to keep everything between them professional and to keep his distance.

That polite, remote relationship of boss and nanny morphed into hot and steamy desire that blasted him. He tried to get his breath as he looked at her.

His eyes had long ago adjusted to the semi-darkness. He could see her wide-eyed stare and the knowledge that she felt the heat between them made his temperature soar higher.

"Erin," he whispered.

"Oh, no…" she whispered with her voice trailing away.

"I've tried. For this whole damn week I've tried to leave you alone, to ignore what I feel, to ignore what you obviously react to. We've both tried. What is so wrong about a simple kiss? I'm not going to steal your heart with a couple of kisses.

"I think your brother has lost all sense of perspective," Cade continued, drawing Erin closer. "I don't want to hurt you, but it seems maybe we've forgotten that kisses can be meaningless fun," he whispered, slipping an arm around her waist while he could feel her pounding pulse in the wrist he still held.

"Erin," he whispered. She turned her face up while both her hands now rested on his forearms.

He leaned down to cover her soft lips. His gentle kiss changed to a demanding, passionate kiss that went deep as his arm tightened around her and he held her close against him.

Instantly, arousal rocked him. Powerful. Undeniable. Too late he realized he had been wrong about her kisses being meaningless fun. She set him on fire and he wanted to kiss her all the rest of the night and through tomorrow. He wanted to make love to her, to seduce her, to never let her go.

As she kissed him back, her mouth was soft, tempting, her tongue an erotic invitation. Her kisses almost buckled his knees and made him hot with desire. He ran his fingers through her soft hair that fell over her nape while he continued to hold her close and kiss her.

"Erin," he whispered, trailing kisses along her throat, down the open V of her sundress, feeling her softness that made him shake with desire. He tried to control it, to hold back, but every move from her only fanned the fire enveloping him.

She pressed against him, her arm holding him tightly. Her other hand stroked his nape, her fingers winding in his hair as she returned his kiss as passionately as he kissed her.

His roaring pulse drowned out all other sounds. Her hips shifted against him and he groaned, wanting her more than he could ever recall wanting any other woman. How could she do this to him? How could her kisses be so spectacular and make him have to struggle to keep from carrying her off to the nearest bedroom?

He should stop, but that was impossible. He knew her kiss wasn't harmless or meaningless, but it also was only a kiss and they couldn't go beyond it. He could continue to kiss for a few more minutes and then he'd have to put an end to the pleasure. He'd have to put the pieces back together afterward because they would have to resume that impersonal nanny and boss relationship.

Right now, though, all he wanted was a beautiful, stunning woman's bone-melting, passionate kisses that were turning his world upside down.

He couldn't keep from running his hand so lightly down her back, feeling her tiny waist and then letting his hand drift lower over the sexy curve of her trim behind, down the back of her thigh that had only the sundress between his fingers and her warm leg.

Her hand closed over his wrist, holding him tightly against her waist until she broke free and stepped back. She released his wrist as she gulped air, trying to get her breath.

"I think we made a mistake, Cade," she whispered. "But it was just once." She gasped for breath as she stared at him without moving. "We can get over that and our kisses won't matter. Kisses that will be forgotten. That's the way it has to be for me to stay here. I'm not risking my heart and you're not interested in anything serious so we both know what has to happen. No more kisses and no flirting. I know you understand."

"It was only kisses, Erin," Cade said. Even as he said the words, he knew their kisses were far from trivial. He'd never had the reaction to kissing a woman that he had with her. Not another woman in his life and he had known some beautiful, sexy women, including one supermodel and one starlet. Both of them should have melted him just from their looks and they had been sexy and exciting, but he couldn't remember their kisses. He knew tonight had been different, far more intense, far more unforgettable. It was the unforgettable part that shook him.

Everything about Erin shook him from the instant she'd opened the door to his office and stepped inside. He should have thanked Luke and hired one of the women from an agency.

He was in deep trouble now. It was taking major willpower to keep from reaching for her to get her back into his arms. With his whole being he wanted to kiss her again.

He couldn't tell how much reaction she was having. She seemed shaken, but she also had just been through a lot of emotional upheaval.

"Erin—" he said, starting to step toward her. She held up her hand.

"Wait a minute, Cade. I want to tell you good-night and go to my suite. You stay right here. We're not walking through the house together. For a few minutes neither one of us used common sense. We're getting back to that. I'll see you in the morning."

She hurried into the house and as he watched her go, he wondered if she'd be able to stick to that vow. He knew there would absolutely never be any getting back to the way they were before their kisses.

Not for him.

Five

Erin rushed to her room, first stopping to check on Amelia and then going to her suite, closing each door as if she could barricade herself from what she felt.

Cade's kisses had shattered what little peace she had gained. She had never responded to any man the way she just had to Cade, which shook her almost as much as the end of her engagement.

Disturbing her even more, she had almost married Adam, who had never made her feel the way Cade just had. She had only worked a week on this job. She was going to be with him for months to come.

She ran her hands through her hair. Why hadn't she listened to her brother and done exactly what he'd said? He had warned her about Cade—warned her that Cade drew women effortlessly.

FREE Merchandise is 'in the Cards' for you!

Dear Reader,

We're giving away FREE MERCHANDISE!

Seriously, we'd like to reward you for reading this novel by giving you **FREE MERCHANDISE** worth over $20 retail. And no purchase is necessary!

You see the Jack of Hearts sticker above? Paste that sticker in the box on the Free Merchandise Voucher inside. Return the Voucher today... and we'll send you Free Merchandise!

Thanks again for reading one of our novels—and enjoy your Free Merchandise with our compliments!

Pam Powers

Pam Powers

P.S. Look inside to see what Free Merchandise is **"in the cards"** for you!

We'd like to send you two free books like the one you are enjoying now. Your two books have a combined price of over $10 retail, but they are yours to keep absolutely FREE! We'll even send you 2 wonderful surprise gifts. You can't lose!

REMEMBER: Your Free Merchandise, consisting of **2 Free Books** and **2 Free Gifts**, is worth over $20 retail! No purchase is necessary, so please send for your Free Merchandise today.

Get TWO FREE GIFTS!

We'll also send you 2 wonderful FREE GIFTS (worth about $10 retail), in addition to your 2 Free books!

Visit us at:
www.ReaderService.com

Books received may not be as shown

FREE MERCHANDISE VOUCHER

2 FREE BOOKS
and
2 FREE GIFTS

Please send my Free Merchandise, consisting of
2 Free Books and **2 Free Mystery Gifts**.
I understand that I am under no obligation to buy
anything, as explained on the back of this card.

225/326 HDL GLUA

Please Print

FIRST NAME

LAST NAME

ADDRESS

APT.#   CITY

STATE/PROV.   ZIP/POSTAL CODE

NO PURCHASE NECESSARY!

HD-N16-FMC15

It wouldn't be a simple matter of avoiding kissing him again. Every inch of her tingled and desire was a raging fire inside. She wanted his kisses, his caresses, his lovemaking—something she wouldn't have dreamed possible when she took the job. She had known she ran a risk to her heart, but she never thought about this hunger for passion. And she couldn't let go and make love without her heart being involved. There was no way sex could ever be casual to her. Her emotions were always tied up in close relationships and intimacy was the strongest emotional tie.

If she didn't guard against more kisses, she would have a giant heartbreak, something she didn't want to go through. Not again. Why hadn't she been more careful?

She shook her head and crossed the room to get ready for bed, but she knew there wouldn't be any sleep for hours.

Every inch of her tingled for Cade's touch, for his hard body pressed against her. She tried to stop thinking about him, placing her fingers against her forehead as if to force out the thoughts.

"Luke, you were right. Oh, you were right. I should have listened," she whispered in the empty room.

Stunned that she had such an intense reaction to Cade, she realized it was probably a reaction to all she had been through. She realized she must be vulnerable to wanting to be loved, to make love, to lose herself in passion that temporarily could drive every vestige of heartache away.

At least she hoped that's all it was. It had been over a year since she had been with Adam, even kissed a man, and there had been no one since him until tonight.

Her reasoning calmed her nerves for about one minute, until she remembered Cade's kisses. Who was she kidding? Her reaction to him wasn't just because of her breakup. It was a physical reaction to the man himself. No other man could simply look at her and make her heart skip a beat. No other man could enter a room and make her pulse jump. No other man could have that effect on her.

It was totally physical, a mutual attraction that she was certain Cade didn't want any more than she did. He was a party guy, never serious, against marriage, unnerved by becoming a guardian. His situation and his attitudes made him the kind of man she planned never to get involved with. Yet she had this intense, heart-pounding reaction to Cade that stopped all her logical thought processes and drove her to do what she knew she would regret.

In his own quiet way Cade was great company. Her brother had always liked him and considered Cade his best friend. Luke trusted Cade and respected him. He also realized how he was about women and long-term relationships.

So why hadn't she heeded Luke's advice?

It wasn't too late. She could get over a kiss. She

needed to keep things in perspective and simply avoid becoming more than his employee.

Could she do that for the next few months with him?

Could she do that with Amelia, as well? Or was she going to get hurt again by people she loved? Little Amelia didn't intend to hurt anyone, but after a few months of caring for her, Erin wondered how much it would hurt to tell Amelia goodbye.

If she wasn't careful Erin knew she was going to lose her heart to Amelia and Cade. Sighing in the darkened bedroom, she decided she was making a mountain out of maybe just an anthill. Not even a molehill.

Hereafter she just had to resist him no matter how difficult it might be. When she put Amelia to bed, she would stay away from Cade the rest of the evening. It was that simple.

She stepped out of bed and pulled a chair to the window. Was Cade sleeping peacefully? For a moment she wished he was in as much turmoil as she was, but then she hoped he slept quietly and had forgotten their kiss and was thinking about who he could ask out next Friday night instead of staying home with his little niece and her nanny. If only he would do that, she might be able to sleep again.

Cade woke and heard Amelia's chatter. He cautiously opened the door to her bedroom. She sat up in her crib and spotted him the minute he cracked open the door. She smiled and held out her arms, babbling incoherent sounds.

He had to laugh as he crossed the room to get her, picking her up. "Aren't you the shameless charmer, using all your wiles to get me to rescue you from that prison of a morning bed? Holding out your arms and looking adorable, babbling cute little sounds that make me want to hug you, smiling at me as if you're not up to something and trying to bribe me with a hug. You look adorable, warm and cuddly. That's shameless, Little Miss Heartbreaker. Of course you got what you wanted—a big strong man to rescue you. A chump who will cater to your every whim and try to find exactly what you would like. You flash that cute smile and gaze at me with those big blue eyes and blow bubbles and get exactly what you want without being able to say one word to me. You don't even know how to point to what you want me to get for you, but somehow you manage to get everyone to give you what you want and do what you want and entertain you, sing to you, read to you, even swim with you."

She laughed as if he had said something very funny to her, making him laugh in turn.

"I think you know you're the cutest little child ever, don't you? I suppose I need to get you changed and dressed. Either that or go wake your nanny, which I would enjoy doing, but not with you in my arms and probably a little on the damp side. You just hang on and be patient and let me find you something comfy to slip into—and I do mean slip into."

Smiling, she made smacking sounds with her lips and he had to laugh.

"You're adorable, Amelia," he said, hugging her and setting her back in the crib. "Let me get you changed here and then later your nanny can fix what I've done."

Twenty minutes later Cade placed Amelia in her high chair and leaned down to look at her as she smiled at him. Yeah, he'd do most anything to make her happy.

Soon he sat facing her, placing her sippy cup with milk on her tray. "I don't know what to feed you. Did you know I made your nanny unhappy last night? You don't know or you wouldn't be nearly this happy with me because you like your nanny. I don't blame you. I like her, too. And she is just flat-out beautiful. And so are you, Little Miss Charmer. Now I'll give you some yummy juice and try to find something you like for breakfast. Okay? And if I don't do so well, your nanny will be out of bed soon and come to your rescue. Or maybe she'll come to my rescue." He laughed at himself. "She's had a long night's sleep… unless she couldn't go to sleep at all. I couldn't and it was all because of your beautiful nanny. What do you think of that?"

He didn't expect the reply he got.

"I think I shouldn't have overheard your very personal conversation."

Cade turned and saw Erin standing in the doorway and his heart skipped. She was in cutoffs and a T-shirt and her hair was up in a ponytail. She looked younger and sexier than ever, and he couldn't keep from letting his gaze drift over a pair of million-dollar legs.

"Lady, you should be a model. Those legs could grace any ad."

"Thank you very much. That improved my morning," she replied, "as well as your one-sided conversation with Amelia."

He grinned and shrugged. "That's what you get for eavesdropping."

"It was far too much fun to stop you. Whew! I'm very flattered."

"You should be, although I could have done better talking to you in person."

"I think we're doing what we each vowed not to do," she said. "Maybe I should go out and come in again and we can both forget everything before that."

"Not on your life, darlin'," he drawled while he fed Amelia a bite.

Relief filled him. Last night when they had parted, Erin was upset and he had been swamped with guilt. This morning he was glad to find her smiling and flirting with him, no longer upset with him.

He glanced over his shoulder to see her moving around the kitchen and he assumed she was getting her breakfast. With her back turned, he took another long look at her legs and inhaled deeply because the air in the room had suddenly become blazing hot. In a moment Erin walked closer as she looked at Amelia.

"You're doing a fine job and she's happy, but I'll relieve you if you'd like."

He glanced at the plate in her hand with a piece of toast and a bowl of fresh berries. "Is that your breakfast?"

"Yes, it is, and I can eat as she eats."

"You go ahead and I'll continue what I'm doing as long as she's happy."

"Don't say I didn't give you a chance. You do pay me to take care of her, you know."

"That's right, but I need to learn how to so when you're not around, I'll know what to do."

"It's pretty simple and it looks as if you're getting the hang of it. Let me know if you want me to take over."

"Thank you. We are doing just fine," he said, giving Amelia some more cereal and smiling as she smacked her lips. "She is a noisy eater."

"She'll grow out of that."

"I hope so before she's a teenager."

"Since when did you get so scared of teenagers? You were one back there in your past, you know."

"I think you're laughing at me again. If you suddenly found yourself the guardian of a teenage boy, wouldn't that shake you?" He glanced at her and shook his head. "Ignore that question. You deal with kids, so it probably wouldn't give you a moment's concern."

"Stop worrying about how you'll be with her more than twelve years from now. That's ridiculous, Cade."

When he looked at it like that, he guessed she had a point. Twelve years was a long time to learn. In the meantime, he'd enjoy raising Amelia, with his nanny's help, of course. Speaking of her nanny…

"Let's get Maisie to stay with Amelia tonight and go out to dinner," he suggested. "You deserve a break."

She laughed. "Thank you, but I think we need to keep everything very professional between the guardian and the nanny."

"And stay here just the two adults in this house after she goes to sleep, intimate and cozy at home where temptation is enormous? That's fine with me," he said.

"We can stay here, two adults in the house who, after putting Amelia to bed, will say good-night to each other early and go our separate ways and remain very professional, very remote and very safely in different parts of your very big ranch house." She took a bite of her toast. "Or better yet, you get a date and go out partying."

"That's what I'm trying to do," he said, gazing at her intently enough to make her blush. Her blush changed the moment for him. He had been joking, lightly flirting with her and having fun with her, but her blush reminded him of their reaction to each other, a physical reaction that he had never experienced with any other woman and one he didn't want to share with her. Worse, he knew she didn't want it, either.

That simple fact made for volatile moments and they came without warning. Like now. He drew a deep breath that didn't calm his racing pulse or stop memories of their kiss last night.

Their gazes had locked and he looked into wide green eyes that conveyed desire no matter how much she fought it.

He tried to conjure up thoughts of her brother. Thinking of Luke had become his cold shower. Instead, memories of holding Erin and kissing her were too vivid and he was becoming aroused, wanting her more with each passing second.

He stood. "I think it's time I take you up on your offer to feed Amelia and get the hell out of the kitchen," he said, his voice thick and deep. He turned and walked away without looking back to see if that was agreeable with her or not. He went down the hall and shut himself into his office, closing the door and letting out his breath. His eyes lit on a small snapshot across the room, one taken years earlier and beginning to fade. He picked it up. In the picture he stood with his arm around Luke's shoulders. Both of them were dusty, their hair tangled. They were dressed in jeans and T-shirts and had been playing ball after school in the neighborhood. Luke wore a grin and they looked like great friends who were having a lot of fun together.

"Buddy, I'm trying," he whispered. "I'll try to avoid her the rest of the weekend, but I wish you were here to keep me on track. You probably don't realize what a gorgeous woman your little sister is. You don't, but I sure do and she's about to wreck my life." He replaced the picture, then walked out. He needed to go to work, to do something physical and get his mind off Erin. He should think of someone to party with tonight. Monday, when Maisie would be back in the house, couldn't come fast enough.

The next weekend Cade made arrangements to stay in Dallas and left Erin at the ranch, paying her extra to stay the weekend. During the week, they went their separate ways after she left to put Amelia to bed. She could see that he was doing all he could to keep away from her, to leave her alone, to learn how to take care of Amelia during the day while Maisie was around. In spite of avoiding being alone as often with Erin, she was more aware of him than ever. The awareness they both felt seemed more intense and she knew he still experienced the same volatile reactions she did.

As two more weeks rolled past, Cade wasn't flirting, and he even tried to avoid staying in the same room with her, and arriving in time to eat with her. But that didn't work, either. She was still aware of him anytime he was near her and missed him when he was not.

On the second Friday in September, rain moved in during midafternoon. Erin got Amelia bathed and changed for dinner, wondering if it would just be the two of them after Maisie left.

Cade had gone out last Saturday night and hadn't returned until late Sunday. She wondered who he had been with and if he would be going out again during the coming weekend.

Even though they saw very little of each other, she couldn't get him out of her thoughts. The brief times they were together, her awareness of him had seemed to increase. Even the slightest brush of fingers caused a disturbing current to run through her. Sometimes she caught him looking intently at her, his blue eyes dark and stormy. When that happened, she wanted to leave the room, but the most she could do was look away.

She tried to avoid thinking about his kisses, remembering, speculating, and she made good on her promise to herself to stay away from him by keeping to her room each night after putting Amelia to bed.

Now, Friday afternoon, as thunder rattled the windowpanes and wind whipped around the house, she wondered where he was and what his plans were for the night. She had told Maisie to go home early so she wouldn't get caught in the rain.

Amelia played with her toys while Erin stood at the window and wondered how much danger Cade was in from lightning or flash flooding.

She watched big drops of rain fall on the patio and into the pool. Then more came and the drops came faster until a sheet of gray rain swept over the house. Lightning flashed and she hoped Cade was safe and dry.

As she stood and watched, her heart skipped a beat when a pickup went past the house and made the turn to pull into the portico on the west side. In seconds, she heard him come in. She fought the inclination to go meet him and ask him about the storm, and then he appeared in the door. His hat was gone, his jeans wet from the knees down.

"I'm glad to see you're back safe," she said.

"Thanks. It's a mess out there." He glanced out the window at the unrelenting storm.

"Are you going out tonight?"

He shook his head. "No, I'm not. We'll manage," he said, giving her a direct look. "I'm going to clean up and then I'll come down. It smells wonderful in here."

"Maisie left a big pot of soup made from a tender roast and she made your favorite—strawberry cake."

"Ahh, an evening at home out of the storm with a great dinner, one of my favorites—a pot of soup and strawberry cake. Can we feed any to Amelia? She'll love it."

"She's too little to crunch down strawberries. Just be patient."

"Too bad. I'll be back shortly and I'll be dry. I think I just made it in the nick of time," he remarked as hail began hitting the house and patio and pool, small white balls of ice bouncing in the yard and tearing leaves from the trees.

As he left, she let out her breath. They would be together until she took Amelia to bed. Till then she'd just have to exercise every ounce of self-control. And self-preservation, she added. Dinner went well, and afterward she sat curled in an easy chair, watching Cade play with Amelia on the floor. He talked to the baby, making faces and noises that made her laugh, picking up a hand puppet to entertain her and she laughed with glee, clapping her hands and reaching for the puppet.

He let her have it and sat watching her play with it. He put it on her hand and showed her how to make it look as if it were talking. She laughed and pulled it off her hand to turn it over and look at it.

He propped Amelia into his lap and leaned back against a chair to stretch his long legs in front of him. After a few minutes, she dropped the puppet and leaned back against Cade, closing her eyes.

"She's getting sleepy. I'll put her to bed," Erin said. "She's had a fun evening with you. You're a good dad, Cade."

"I'm trying. She makes it easy to be a good dad. I already love her with all my heart and want to try to do the best I can." He kissed the top of her head. "I'll take her to bed. I'm learning and getting better at this."

"Yes, you are," Erin answered, amused by his insecurity in this one area of his life when he was so confident in things so much more difficult.

"Sit back and enjoy yourself. Watch the rain," he said, turning a lamp off so the lighting was softer. "Our creeks will be up, but I hope that's the only result of this storm. It isn't a real problem. The creeks rise and sometimes flood and cover the bridges, but we aren't usually cut off." A wave of heavy rain hit the house again. "I'm glad to be home tonight." He stood, holding Amelia with great care.

"I should take her and go on to my suite."

"It's a stormy night and we could lose power. Why

don't you stay and we can talk or play a game if you prefer. I'll stay on my side of the room like always. That should be safe."

"Nothing is safe," she said quietly and then waved her hand. "See, I shouldn't have said that."

"I'm glad you did. Relax, we're adults. Our kissing was not life-threatening or life-changing and we don't ever have to kiss again," he said, looking down at Amelia in his arms. "You stay. I'll be back and when I return, I don't want to have to sit down here in the rain all alone. Now I'll take her to bed and if I need help, I'll call you on the monitor."

She smiled at him. "Yes, sir," she replied. He grinned, glanced again at Amelia, who was breathing deeply as she slept. Erin quietly watched him carry Amelia out of the room.

When he returned, he sat in the easy chair across the room from her, as promised. He looked relaxed, sexy and way too appealing. She should have gone with Amelia, but it was fun to sit with Cade instead of spending a lonely evening in her room. Sometimes she didn't mind, but some nights she wanted to be with him and tonight was one. She'd give herself an hour with him and then she'd retire.

"Cade, you're so good with Amelia," she said, thinking about him with the little girl and his feelings about marriage. "Why in the world are you so opposed to marriage?" Erin asked and then blinked. "I'm sorry—that's a personal question you don't have to answer. It's just that I've heard Luke talk about how opposed you are to marriage."

"I figured you knew because your brother does," he said, stretching out his long legs again to cross them at the ankles. He still had his boots kicked off and he wiggled his toes.

"It's because of my dad's rotten marriages," he explained. "I've seen firsthand how unhappy marriage can be and I've seen little firsthand how happy and good it can be. I saw that when I stayed at your house because your folks have a good, happy marriage from what I know. It seems the luck of the draw to end up happily married and I never want to come out on the losing side and get caught in what my folks had."

"That's sad," she said, frowning as she heard from him a little more about his feelings on marriage and his reasons behind his determination to stay a lifelong bachelor. "You're such a good daddy for Amelia."

"Thanks. That's reassuring because I still feel very unsure of myself with her, but it's a little less worrisome."

Erin's gaze drifted down the long length of him and she felt a tingle. She remembered being in his arms. "You know that's a foolish reason to reject marriage. What your dad did doesn't have a thing to do with the way you'll be," she said. "You're a different man."

"I'm his son. We have the same blood in our veins. I'm scared I'll turn out the way he was. He was in love with all three women before he married them. Even if I don't turn out like my dad, marriage doesn't look like a happy, positive arrangement. I know it is in your family, but I don't want to take that chance. I'll admit, my dad was exceptionally lousy at being a husband and dad—not speaking to his firstborn is a classic example and I would never do anything like that. But marriage seems a huge chance to take, like an amateur trying to cross Niagara Falls on a tightrope. It might work out great and one would have all sorts of attention and laurels. Or you might just fall in and drown."

"That's a gloomy outlook. Can't you see that you're not the kind of father your dad was? It's not something that is inherited or contagious."

"I grew up around him. I hated the fights my parents had. I hated the way he might come home for holidays or he might not. We never knew. He really didn't care about us. He was around some and we got some of his attention, whereas Blake was totally ignored, but all I remember were fights between my parents. I don't know how many nights as a kid I was in bed and would hold my hands over my ears to keep from listening to them and I would vow that I'd never get married."

"That's the view of a child. You probably won't be one little bit like him and you're cutting yourself out of a wonderful life filled with love and joy. I can't imagine life without children in it. Remember her sitting on your lap. She was happy and she likes you and goes to you and holds her arms out for you to take her. Would your dad have done that?"

"Hell, no. I don't know what he did when I was her age, but I never saw him do that with Gabe."

"Don't you want your own kids?"

"One is probably all I can cope with. And as long as we're on this subject and getting personal, I'm sorry for your breakup. I wish you didn't have to go through that, and I wish you the best and lots of luck in the future."

"Thank you," she said quietly. "I still want marriage and a family. Not now, of course, but someday. Adam broke our engagement because I couldn't guarantee I would give him biological children."

"Maybe you're better off without Adam."

"I'm beginning to think I am. I'm sure Luke told you I had a miscarriage and I might not be able to carry a baby to full term. That's very important to some people. It isn't to me. I'll probably adopt my family and that's fine with me." She paused when she got a bit emotional, then added, "That breakup wasn't long ago and I'm still trying to get beyond it."

"As long as we're giving each other marital advice, I've got something to say," he remarked drily and she had to smile, knowing she had started this, so she had to listen to whatever he was going to tell her she should do. "If a guy really loves you, he'll still want to marry you even if you can't give him biological children. As you said, you can adopt."

"Thank you, Mr. Marriage Counselor," she said, smiling at him and trying to avoid thinking about what he just said. "I agree and I brought that bit of advice on myself."

"Yes, you did. I'm as qualified as you are to give marital advice."

"No, you're not," she teased. "You've never been engaged, so I've come closer to actually marrying."

He got up and crossed the room to her, to place his hands on both sides of her chair. "That gives you a little experience, but I've got a lot because I spent fifteen years growing up in a bad marriage until my folks divorced," he said, leaning closer as he talked. "That makes my advice more valid."

"You were going to stay on your side of the room tonight," she warned him.

"See—this is why I shouldn't marry. I don't do what I say I will." His eyes darkened. "Scared of me?"

"Not in the least. I have no intention of marrying you," she said, knowing he was joking. "Now go back to your side of the room and think about my brother."

Cade took her hand to pull her to her feet. "I want to know something else. Give me a straight answer," he said, and her pulse jumped. "I've had time to catch up on the sleep I missed the night after our first kiss. Did you miss any sleep?"

"Cade, we weren't going to do this," she said, suddenly solemn, knowing they had moved beyond teasing and joking about their backgrounds. His probing blue eyes held desire.

"I think you just answered my question," he said in a husky voice as his gaze lowered to her mouth and she tingled in expectation.

For fleeting seconds she knew she should move. Now was the moment to step away from him, but she couldn't. The past year her life had been tough and filled with hurt and loneliness and a lot of hard work. For a few minutes, how disastrous would it be to enjoy some pleasure and excitement? How much could a few more kisses and another sleepless night hurt?

Six

Common sense reared its ugly head. It whispered in her ear—*No*, it screamed, *walk away!* She tried her best to ignore it, instead gazing into his blue eyes that held such desire, she trembled. Still, that voice of reason echoed in her ears.

"Cade," she whispered. "I—I need to go," she said, trying to stay safe, but filled with wanting him.

"I'm not holding you," he whispered in return, kissing her throat and then her ear, light kisses that made her want to wrap her arms around him and pull him close.

Just walk away.

When his tongue caressed her neck, she sighed. If she wasn't careful, his mouth would have her melting right here at his feet. She leaned into his kiss and again the question nagged at her. Would a few little kisses really compound her hurt? She ached to be in his arms, to kiss and be kissed. Could she do that and still keep her heart intact?

She knew better than to fall in love with him, but could she guard her heart against that and still kiss him? Torn between desire and caution, she stood up from the chair while an inner debate raged. He stood mere inches from her, but she already felt his loss. Her head told her to turn and leave him. But she stood rooted to the spot.

Beneath his cheer and friendliness and care of his little niece, beyond his sexy appeal, Cade was cynical and had closed his heart to love. She wanted a long-term relationship—total commitment at some point. She wanted a family like her own. Cade had grown up wanting to avoid the lifestyle she longed for.

He wrapped his arms around her and tilted her chin up so that her eyes met his. She saw the heat in their dark blue depths. "Stop battling yourself," he whispered, his mouth a hairbreadth away from hers. "You know you want to kiss me. You know you liked when we kissed. Just give in to it." He brushed her lips with his and it was like spark to tinder. Her heart pounding, she wrapped her arms around his neck and wound her fingers in his thick short hair at the back of his head.

In spite of all her arguments, in spite of their first kisses and the misery later, she couldn't walk away. She wanted him too much.

His strong arms pulled her flush against him and he took her mouth hard, his tongue going deep.

So inflamed with desire, she could only hold him tightly and kiss him back. She had crossed an invisible line and at the moment she didn't care. She didn't want to go back. Saying goodbye to caution and logic, she thrust her hips against him, finding him hard, aroused, ready to love her.

"Cade," she whispered before his mouth covered hers again and his tongue stroked hers as he held her tightly, his arm a steel band around her waist while his other hand trailed lightly over her curves, moving over her back and down over her bottom, stirring her desire. Her heart pounded and she kissed him eagerly.

He caressed her so lightly in scalding strokes that made her want more. Now that she had let go, she wanted no barriers between them. She wanted to run her hands over his naked skin, wanted to touch and kiss him everywhere. He must have felt the same, because before she knew it, his fingers were at her buttons and then he pushed the top of her dress off her shoulders and it fell around her waist.

She gasped with pleasure as he cupped her naked breasts in his large hands, caressing her, sending streaks of fire to the part of her that ached for him.

As he kissed her, she pulled his shirt free. Her fingers trembled, and he stilled them, yanking his knit shirt over his head in one smooth motion and tossing it aside. He leaned forward to kiss her again, needing her lips on his.

Wanting to explore his marvelous body, she ran

her hands over his chest, feeling the curly chest hair beneath her fingers. Her fingers traced solid muscles, lean sinew, then the smooth skin of his upper arms. Finally she wrenched her mouth from his and let it follow the path her fingers had taken. She dragged her lips across his throat and chest.

Groaning, he gripped her head in his hands and pulled her back for another dizzying kiss. She was so overwhelmed with desire that she could only cling to him, close her eyes and be swept along. Until Cade, she hadn't been kissed in so long. If she could ever call what she'd experienced before a kiss. Not after this man.

Running her hands across his strong shoulders, she moaned with pleasure as he caressed her, his callused hands moving lightly to heighten desire. He swung her into his arms, never breaking contact, and carried her to the sofa where he sat with her on his lap as he continued to run his hand over her and caress her. When she raised her head and looked into his blue eyes, there was no mistaking that he wanted her.

He slipped his hands beneath the full cotton skirt of her sundress. His hands were warm as they trailed up her thighs in light, tingling caresses that made her open her legs and sit astride him.

He cupped her breasts again, his tanned hands dark against her pale, soft skin while he leisurely kissed first one breast and then the other, causing streaks of pleasure that rocked her. Closing her eyes, she clung to his muscled arms.

"You're beautiful," he whispered, "so beautiful."

He kissed her mouth and then leaned down to run his tongue around her nipple.

She knew in a few more minutes they would never want to stop. A few more minutes, a few more kisses and tender touches, and she'd surrender to total seduction. Could she? She slipped off his lap, turning away and gasping for breath.

"Cade, I'm not ready for this," she whispered.

He didn't answer and she wondered whether or not he heard her. His hands folded lightly on her shoulders as he kissed her ear and then lifted her hair away to brush kisses on her nape.

She twisted to face him and he held her lightly with his hands on her waist. "We'll stop. I don't want to push you where you don't want to go," he whispered as he continued showering light kisses on her throat, her ear. All the time he kissed her, his hand caressed her breast, first one and then the other.

She wanted him with all her being, and trembled, debating if she could cope with the consequences if they made love tonight. "I want you," she whispered, "but I don't want more hurt."

"I understand," he said, between kisses. He turned her to face him and bent down to lave her breast, his tongue drawing lazy circles around the tip while his hand pulled up her skirt and nestled between her thighs.

"I don't want to hurt you in any way," he whispered. "Stop when you want. You're beautiful, darlin'. I want to kiss you and touch you all night long, but only, only if you want me to."

She thought about her life. She had been alone since her breakup over a year ago. Until Cade, it had been over a year since she had been kissed or held and loved or had any emotional ties to a man. Not that she would have any deep, long-lasting ties with this committed bachelor. But she wanted him nonetheless. Wanted the passion that he inspired, the pleasure that only he could give her.

There was no denying that he was desirable. That he stirred her more than any other man ever had, including the one she had been engaged to marry. Could she deny herself one night with him?

She framed Cade's face with her hands and gazed into his blue eyes that held blatant desire. "I want you," she whispered.

He held her tighter and she swore she saw flames ignite in his eyes.

"I want to make love, Cade, but I don't have any protection."

"I have protection." He cupped her face in his strong hands. "I want to make love to you all night long if that's what you want," he said, slipping his arm around her waist to draw her against him as he leaned down to kiss her, another intense, passionate kiss that made her feel as if he loved her more than anyone or anything on the earth. "Erin, I don't want to hurt you."

She nodded. "I know you don't. I also know we don't want the same things." She responded to Cade as she had never responded to any other man, and right now nothing could stop her from making love with him. But she knew theirs could only be a brief affair before she said goodbye and she'd have to forget him. Was she rushing into another situation where she would be heartbroken?

For this night, this moment, she didn't care. She wanted to make love, to yield to seduction, to grasp joy and life and loving here where it was incredible with him. The moment could be lost and never come again and she chose consequences over regrets.

"Cade, make love to me," she whispered.

It was all the invitation he needed.

He showered kisses on her while his hands drifted up her thighs, caressing her between her legs, stroking her so lightly that she opened to give him access.

He picked her up to carry her to his bedroom, knelt to place her on the mattress. He slipped her sundress over her legs, and then, starting at her ankle, he trailed kisses lightly over every inch of her skin. His breath was warm, his tongue wet, exciting, sensual on her as he moved slowly up, till he met the flimsy fabric of her panties. He slid them down, torturously slow, stopping to caress her here and there, then tossed them aside. He knelt before her and placed her legs over his broad shoulders so he could stroke and love her with his lips and tongue. He took his time, until she was writhing beneath him, her hands fluttering over him.

She cried out, writhing, wanting to kiss him in turn the way he did her. His tongue stroked her relentlessly, making her cry out with need, nearly taking her to the point of no return.

But she didn't want to come like this. Not before she had her taste of him.

With a gasp, she pushed him back. "Let me kiss you the way you kiss me," she said. She slid down his body, her naked breasts rubbing against him, her tongue trailing over his flat, male nipples, until she caressed his manhood.

Then she knelt over him to torment him the way he had her. Her mouth took him in and he groaned. She ran her tongue over him, loving him, and loving each sigh and moan that he emitted. When she felt his body tighten beneath her, he stopped her. Taking her into his arms, he rolled her over, so he was above her. His hands combed into her hair and he gazed down at her, looking into her eyes with a need that made her shake. No man had ever looked at her as if he wanted to devour her and could never get enough of her.

"Cade," she gasped, trying to draw him down to her, to pull him closer so she could hold him against her heart. His dark blue eyes held a need that made her tremble and feel she was the only woman on earth for him.

"Ahh, darlin', you're beautiful," he whispered, a hoarse remark she could barely hear between kisses. "We'll take our time. I want to love you for hours." He ran his hands through her hair.

She couldn't get enough of this man. As if a dam had burst inside, she poured out every drop of passion and the physical expression of her feelings, knowing that Cade was special and this night was unique and then she would have to let it all go. For tonight, he was here in her arms and she could kiss and touch him and try to give him the pleasure he was giving her.

"Kiss me," she whispered.

And he did. A kiss that was hard and passionate. A kiss that told her she had made another monumental mistake with him. Because making love with Cade could never just be once. For her, it was more than a brief fling. He made her feel as if he had offered his body and his heart. She knew better, but that was what she felt and she was in deeper than she dreamed she would be. There was no undoing or turning back now.

She watched him as he opened a drawer in a bedside chest and withdrew a condom. Relishing every moment with him, she watched him put it on and move between her legs. He looked virile, ready to love and incredibly sexy.

She started to sit up, to throw her arms around his neck. Instead, he pushed her to the bed and came down to kiss her, another hot, passionate kiss that made her want him more than ever. "Cade," she whispered. "I want you. Now."

When he lowered his weight, slowly filling her, she gasped with pleasure.

"Put your legs around me," he murmured, and she did as he asked, running her hands down his muscled back and over his hard bottom, tugging him closer to her.

He filled her, hot and hard, moving deliberately as she arched beneath him. She started to cry out, but his mouth covered hers and her cry was muffled. He partially withdrew, driving her need higher, only to thrust into her again and carry her to new heights. Over and over. She held him tightly, giving herself completely to him, giving him complete access to her as she clasped her ankles around his waist. Need pounded in her, until with one final, deep thrust she climaxed. And he followed her. They rocked together as ecstasy overwhelmed her.

But Cade was not done. Minutes later he moved inside her again, slowly at first, then faster, harder, deeper. She thought she was spent, but of their own volition her hips rose to meet his and she was struck with a second shuddering release. Only then did his control finally shatter.

Clinging to him she kept with him, her head thrashing while she held him tightly with her long legs locked around his narrow waist.

"Cade," she whispered. Her fingers dug into his shoulders, and then she ran her hand down his back and over his bottom. Crying out, she was enveloped in rapture.

He shuddered with his release and they pumped together until spent. Euphoria became an invisible cloud wrapping them in a momentary closeness that made them one.

"So wonderful," he whispered, kissing her temple lightly, and she turned her head to kiss him, a long, slow kiss that was satisfaction and union.

Gasping for breath, she hugged him as he held her with his arms wrapped around her and their legs entwined. Gradually their breathing returned to normal. He rolled over, taking her with him and holding her close while he combed her hair gently from her face. "Ahh, darlin', so good, so good," he whispered.

"For a moment I want to hold you. You're strong and solid and sure, all good things that are missing in my life right now."

"No, they're not," he said quietly. "Erin, you're strong and you've been through a lot and you got through it and are moving on. That's strong. You're solid because you know what you want and you're pursuing it and you've picked up the pieces. You're sure because you have confidence in yourself and in your future. They're not missing at all." He kissed the tip of her nose. "But I'm more than happy for you to hold me for the rest of the night if you want. You are a fantastic woman and I'm glad I know you."

"I'm glad, too," she said.

The moment had become more serious and brought reality back. She ran her hands over his shoulder and chest, drawing her fingers lightly through the smattering of chest hair, refusing to think about consequences, choices or even tomorrow morning or the decision she had made tonight.

She was in Cade's arms after the most fantastic sex possible. Lovemaking that had been wild and passionate and fulfilling. She still floated in a euphoria that shut away all the problems in her life. Before she knew it, the bubble would burst and real life would come crashing down to envelope her soon enough, but for a bit more time she was in Cade's arms, still tingling from his caresses and hot, passionate loving.

As she snuggled against him, he brushed another light kiss on her forehead. "This is good, just to hold you close," he said. Beneath her fingers on his chest, she could feel the faint vibrations when he talked.

"I don't want to move."

"I don't want you to move. And I don't want to move, either. This is the perfect place to be." After a few minutes, he shifted on his side, holding her close while she faced him. She combed unruly waves of thick black hair from his forehead. "I'll bet you were a cute little boy." She had no idea where that thought came from. The body before her was all man.

"I was adorable," he said, his blue eyes twinkling.

She laughed. "And probably spoiled rotten as the oldest child."

"Me? Spoiled? Never," he drawled, and they smiled at each other. He trailed light kisses on her temple and rubbed her back lightly as he held her. They were quiet and she felt enveloped in bliss.

"For a while, you made all the problems go away," she whispered. "I know they'll come back because they're real and part of my life, but for the past hour they ceased to exist."

"That's what's meant to be. Sex is magic. It's the icing on life's cake," he said quietly between light kisses.

"So I'm dessert," she remarked drily.

"Definitely," he said, kissing away her laugh. He leaned back after a moment and with his fingers, moved strands of her long hair away from her face. She was still on her side in his arms and she gazed up at him as she ran her hands lightly over his chest and along his muscled arm.

"Cade, this is an intimate moment, a brief time I feel closer to you than I ever have. I'm not pushing for myself because I know I'm going out of your life soon, but I—I wish you'd rethink your views on marriage. You're going to be a wonderful dad for Amelia. You're not like your father."

"Thank heaven for that one," he remarked. "I'm glad for your great faith in me. I'm not as scared to be with her, but right now, I think it's because I know you're here to save me."

She gazed up at him, at the faint shadow of stubble on his jaw. The point was not lost on her that he didn't address her comment. She decided not to push. Not right now.

They became quiet. Wrapped in his arms she refused to think further about the future, or the past. For the next few hours, only tonight existed and she intended to enjoy every moment of it.

"Cade, I didn't know sex could be so good," she whispered.

He smiled. "I'm glad you said that because that's what I was thinking," he said.

She smiled at him, but didn't believe he had been thinking any such thing.

He tightened his arm around her to draw her close and brush light kisses on her forehead. "Ahh, darlin'. This is so good. Stay right here in my arms and let me hold you all night," he said.

She nodded, agreeable to do exactly that. She made

her choice tonight and it was done. She stopped thinking and let him pull her close against him.

"So very sexy," he whispered.

She held him tightly as if she had caught happiness for a moment and could hang on to it. But she knew better than to think her happiness was tied up in Cade.

"Will you go out with me next Friday night? We could prevail on Maisie to watch Amelia."

"Shh. Let's not talk about next week or tomorrow or anything beyond the next few hours. And no, we're not going out together."

"Okay, only now and the next few hours. Come closer. You're way too far away," he said, nuzzling her and she giggled.

"I don't think you could get a sheet of paper between us. I'm as close as I can get."

"Are you really? Let me see," he teased, running his hands lightly between them, his fingers drifting over her, squeezing lightly.

"Satisfied?"

"Mmm, ever so, but a repeat performance might be in the wings," he said. "How about we get in my hot tub and soak and talk and see what happens?"

"You know exactly what will happen and I can't wait," she drawled, and he grinned as he stood and picked her up. Holding her in his arms he kissed her. "I could get used to this really fast," he said.

"Well, don't get too used to it. This is tonight only. I told you, let's just think of now and a few hours from now."

"Of course," he said, carrying her into his bathroom and taking the iPad so they could monitor the nursery.

In minutes they were seated in a hot tub of water as they talked about general topics, the ranch, subjects that were harmless and didn't involve families and the future.

She leaned back against Cade, feeling his muscles flex when he moved. He was warm, hard, wet, all sensations that were sexy and made her think of making love again.

It was almost an hour before he stepped out of the tub and handed her a thick towel. He began to gently dry her and in minutes she was in his arms while they kissed and he carried her back to his big bed.

When she stirred in the first pale light as dawn spilled into the room, Cade drew her into his arms to kiss her and she was lost again to lovemaking. She knew it would end, but night had not completely gone and she felt still captured in the magic of their lovemaking.

It was a sunny morning when she slipped away on her own to shower and dress in jeans and a blue cotton shirt. She braided her hair and by the time she finished Amelia was awake.

They would have the weekend to themselves, just the three of them, and Erin suspected tonight would be a repeat of Friday night which was all right with her. She had given herself over to making love this weekend, even though she knew living with Cade created an emotional risk that would be a real threat to her heart.

She paused in changing Amelia and stood there staring into space as she thought about the past hours in Cade's arms.

She hoped she wasn't already falling in love with him. When she was in the house with him, having made love all night, it was difficult to think about hurting or missing him. Right now, she hoped she could walk away in mid-December with her heart intact. One weekend should not be impossible to get over.

Beyond one weekend, it would be a giant risk. She hoped she hadn't miscalculated and put her heart in jeopardy already. Her response to Cade was different from any other man she had known. That was a warning to take care or she would lose her heart to him and hurt more than she had with the broken engagement.

Amelia stirred, kicking out her feet and calling Erin's attention. She focused on her little charge.

"Hey, little sweetie," she said to Amelia who smiled. "Are you ready for a fun day?" She finished changing her diaper and snapped her pajamas. "Let me brush your hair," she said, working the soft baby brush through her black curls.

"You're a sweet baby. Are you going to make me love you? Am I going to love you and fall in love with your uncle? I can't do that, sweetie, so don't be too adorable. Don't make me miss you every day after I leave here. I want to be able to tell you and your uncle goodbye and not feel as if my heart is being ripped out and locked away here on this Texas ranch." Amelia was paying no attention to her, looking instead at her own toes, seemingly mesmerized by them.

"You'll get a bath after breakfast. In the meantime, let's go to the kitchen. Okay?"

Amelia babbled in reply. She seemed to be enjoying the morning and happy to listen to Erin talk to her. When she carried Amelia to the kitchen, Cade was cooking and had breakfast almost ready.

He turned to put down a spatula, wash and dry his hands and cross the room to Amelia. "How's my baby girl?" he asked as she held out her arms and he took her. "Don't you look pretty this morning? Your nanny has your pretty hair combed and you look adorable." He put her in her chair, glancing back at Erin. "She doesn't cry as often since you joined us. Congratulations on that one. I'm glad because when she cries, I panic and wonder what's disturbing her."

Erin had to bite back a smile at the thought of Cade getting panicky over Amelia crying. "Cade, babies do cry and the world isn't coming to an end, and sometimes when they cry it's just because of nothing more than they're hungry, wet, tired or teething."

"Yeah, common sense tells me that, but I can't bear for her to cry because she can't tell me why. That's what's so scary and—" He stopped, then walked up close to her to look intently at her, as if seeing her for the first time. "She's not the only one looking pretty this morning. You're gorgeous, Erin," he said, trailing his finger along her cheek.

"Thank you." She ignored the thrill that sent goose

bumps down her arms. "Are you going to work today?" she asked.

"I am because we have a tree that fell on a fence and a bridge over a creek to repair. First I'll feed Amelia and then I'll help you clean this kitchen. In the meantime, you can eat your breakfast undisturbed."

"Sure. You're free to go at any time and I'll take over Amelia and the kitchen chores."

He turned to Amelia, so Erin got her breakfast and sat eating it while he talked to Amelia and fed her. Later, he shooed Erin out of the kitchen while he cleaned and she bathed and changed Amelia, playing with her in the sitting room. She was winding up a musical jack-in-the-box for Amelia when she heard Cade's boots and looked up to see him standing in the doorway. Her pulse jumped and she wanted to walk into his arms.

He had on a jeans jacket and his broad-brimmed black hat was pushed to the back of his head, framing his face. He looked like a handsome, sexy rancher and she hoped he told her goodbye and left because she wouldn't be able to resist him if he wanted to kiss before he left.

"I'm gone. It's raining again. I have my phone. If you need anything, Harold is nearby and his number is posted by the phone. Just call and he'll be here right away."

"I'll be fine and so will Amelia. You take care. You'll be out in the elements."

"I'll come home to a hot dinner and a warm house

and dare I hope, maybe hugs and kisses. Think about that one today."

"Cade, we've been very careful and I don't want to get too involved."

"Let's rethink that one," he said in a deeper, quieter voice, shrugging away from the doorjamb and crossing the kitchen to her, making her pulse quicken again. He placed his hands on her shoulders and she couldn't get her breath. How could he make her melt with a look?

He glanced beyond her at Amelia happily playing with a rag doll. "Stop being afraid of life, Erin," he murmured. "Let go and live a little so you can get what you want out of life," he added, and her heart thudded as she looked into his blue eyes.

"Watch out," she whispered. "I might take your advice."

"Be good if you did," he answered, but desire filled his expression and she didn't think he knew what he replied. He wrapped his arm around her waist, pulled her close and covered her mouth with his.

Her heart slammed against her ribs and the protest she was beginning to think about died instantly. His words echoed in her mind. *"Let go and live a little so you can get what you want..."*

Closing her eyes, she wrapped her arms around his neck and returned his kiss.

Kissing her hard and passionately, he leaned over her, making her heart pound and her pulse drum in her ears. He released her abruptly and she opened her eyes to find him watching her.

"That's better, darlin'," he said and pushed his hat squarely on his head as he turned and left the kitchen. In seconds she heard the back door close, and in a few more minutes his pickup motor started and then faded as he drove away.

Her heart pounded and she tingled all over, wanting to be in his arms, wanting his kisses more than ever, remembering every minute of the night. Were they going to have another long night of lovemaking tonight? Could she resist him? Did she want to resist him? Was he right in telling her to let go and live a little so she could get what she wanted? Maybe she should take his advice.

Cade left to work on a fence that was down from the storm that swept through the area during the night. The wind had been high and broken tree limbs had fallen on fences. He knew his men were scattered on the ranch, moving cattle to other grazing areas and cutting up limbs, hauling them away to clear the area and repairing the bridge, repairing another string of fences and setting up new posts. Working automatically as he cut limbs and then loaded debris into his truck when necessary, he was lost in thoughts about the night.

Making love to Erin had been the best ever—a shocking and unexpected discovery. Along with the most fantastic sex, however, had come a truckload of guilt.

He had promised Luke to look out for his baby sister and then turned around and seduced her. She was vulnerable, hurting still from losses, and he hadn't kept his word, something he couldn't recall ever doing in his life. He definitely had never done it to Luke. He hadn't been true to Luke and he hated that part of what he had done.

Taking off his hat, he wiped his brow with his sleeve. "Dammit," he said quietly. He had always been able to maintain control. What had happened to his self-control?

It had gone flying away the moment he kissed Erin. The one time in his life when self-control was needed badly. He groaned and wanted to gnash his teeth. Erin, of all the women he had known, the little sister of his best friend. He hadn't paid a lick of attention to her when she was a little kid. How he wished he had continued to see her in the same way now that she was grown.

He thought about kissing her, momentarily losing himself in memories that made him hot and temporarily took away his regrets. He would lose Luke's friendship if or when Luke discovered what Cade had done, because he'd broken a trust with his life-long buddy. It wouldn't matter that the lady was ready and willing, too. It wouldn't matter one tiny bit. Luke meant what he said and he always stuck by what he said. Cade had solid proof of that in the past. And he couldn't blame Luke for being angry when he found out.

Cade propped his foot on a thick oak branch that had fallen and thought about Erin. The worst part of all of this wasn't his guilt or the end of a friendship.

What was even worse—he still wanted to go to bed with her. He wanted to make love to her even more than he had last night. The damage was already done to Luke's friendship, that was over and there was no way he would ever get it back.

Maybe if he and Erin were wildly in love everything would be all right with Luke, but they weren't in love. Erin was still all bottled up emotionally and he wasn't a man to fall in love.

She would be gone all too soon in mid-December and once she left, he doubted he would ever see her again.

He hoped with all his heart that Erin had no lasting effects from their lovemaking except good ones. He was certain that during the hours they loved and had been together, she had briefly lost that perpetual hurt that she carried. Time would heal her wounds— at least the broken engagement. Erin was too involved with children and liked them too much to ever completely heal over the loss of her baby. That was in the category of his losing Nate and Lydia. Although he'd had years with Nate, it still was a heartbreaking and permanent loss.

At least he was beginning to catch on how to care for Amelia and eventually, they would start the search for a new nanny.

Again guilt stabbed him. "Sorry, buddy," he said aloud, thinking about Luke and knowing he had broken a trust. If Erin really hurt over their parting, Luke would be able to guess why.

"Dammit," Cade said, unable to fully concentrate

on something as mundane as clearing the broken tree limbs and stringing more barbed wire, plus driving in some fence posts. He should have kept a few guys to work with him instead of sending them to different places on the ranch, because clearing limbs and driving posts were a lot easier with four hands than with two.

He leaned on a posthole digger and stared into space and saw only Erin's green eyes, her long hair spilling over her bare shoulders. When they had the evening to themselves later, he wanted her in his arms. Forgetting where he was, Cade thought about her kisses. When he realized he was lost in fantasies about Erin, he turned back to the wire he would string. But in seconds she commandeered his thoughts once again. He shook his head. What kind of spell had she woven with him? When had there been a woman in his life who interfered with what he needed to get done, who captured his thoughts and imagination? Of all the women he had known—the one it shouldn't be was Erin. He groaned and started digging, throwing himself into the job and working as hard and fast as possible, trying to dig her out of his thoughts as he did the earth. How important was she becoming to him? He dismissed that question as ridiculous. She would soon say goodbye and they wouldn't see each other again unless Luke fell in love and married and they crossed paths at the wedding. And that was not likely to happen, at least in the foreseeable future, because Luke was in love with his work.

Cade pulled out his phone, made a call and put his

phone back into his pocket. Soon a pickup appeared with three cowboys who came to help.

It was twenty minutes of working alongside his hands before he realized he had paused and was lost in thought about Erin. Startled, he returned to digging furiously. Why couldn't he get her out of his thoughts? A far more persistent question—would she let him make love to her again tonight?

Seven

That night Erin rocked Amelia, finally tucking the sleeping baby into her bed and tiptoeing to her room, closing the door between them because the monitor was on. She turned and faced Cade. He stood in the open door to the hall and she walked into the sitting room to see why. Her heartbeat raced and she wanted to walk into his arms and kiss him.

Cade straightened and approached her. Day by day he was becoming more important, more exciting. When she had to tell him goodbye, she didn't want to look back with regrets.

"I was afraid you'd stay up here without coming back. Let's sit and talk," he said.

Wanting to be with him, she nodded. "Sure," she said and saw the flare of satisfaction in his blue eyes.

He closed the last bit of space between them. "Before we go back to the sitting room…" He slipped his arm around her waist. "This has been a long day and I feel as if we've been apart for a long time," he said. The moment his arm went around her, her heart thudded.

"Cade," she whispered before his mouth covered hers. She held him tightly and kissed him passionately while he picked her up.

He carried her to his suite and sat on his sofa, cradling her against his shoulder, holding her tightly with one arm around her while he caressed her.

She moaned with pleasure, running her hands over him and wanting him more than ever, and with a sense of urgency that she could only assume from his touches he also felt. All the longings she had experienced all day poured out and she kissed him hungrily.

Clothes were flung aside and her hands shook in her haste. She wanted him and was ready to make love to him again. He returned her kisses while his hands moved all over her, pausing only to slip on protection. Then he lifted her over him. As he lowered her onto his thick rod and they moved together in a pounding rhythm, she locked her long legs around him. Crying out, she held him tightly while release shook her and he reached a shuddering climax.

Showering kisses on her face and shoulders and throat, he carried her to his bed, yanked back covers and placed her on the bed to stretch beside her and pull her into his embrace.

"I've wanted you with all my being," he whispered, stroking her damp hair away from her forehead. "All day long you've been in my thoughts and I couldn't wait to be alone with you tonight."

She showered light kisses on his throat and shoulder, stroking him with her long fingers. "Soon I'll be gone and what we have together will be over as it should be, and as both of us want it to be. You're not into permanence and I am—it's that simple."

"That's true, but I want you in my bed and in my arms until you go. Will you move in here until you leave?"

She thought about his question. "No. If Luke would learn that I have, you'd lose a friend no matter what I said. No, I won't move in. I don't want to leave here with a broken heart, either, and if I'm with you that much, I'll fall in love and a broken heart is what will happen. I can't take an affair lightly. You can't take one seriously." She framed his face with her hands to look directly into his dark blue eyes.

"Someday you'll meet someone and fall in love and you'll want marriage—at least I hope you do for your sake and Amelia's. When that happens, you'll be a good husband and a good dad because you're a good man. From what you've told me, you're not like your father. You've told me not to be afraid to live—you shouldn't, either," she said and brushed a light kiss on his cheek.

"Thanks for the vote of confidence," he said, his voice hoarse as it usually became when he was aroused.

"I'll stay as long as I agreed, until mid-December, but I want you to hire another nanny soon and let me help her get settled in. I think the transition would be better for Amelia. She has a lot of new people in her life and she's adjusted well, but hiring a nanny sooner while I'm here will help them get to know each other," she said.

Cade frowned as she finger-combed his black hair back off his forehead. Her hand trailed down over his muscled shoulder, moving lower across his hard chest. "You think that's best?"

"I think it's best for all concerned. I think Amelia will adjust more easily and I think I will be less likely to leave my heart behind when I go. I can start letting the other nanny spend time with Amelia and we'll have her with us in the evening and that will help also."

"I don't see how in sweet hell that will help anything except the new nanny's income. You don't want to be here with me? You don't want to be here in my arms? That isn't what you've indicated in the past hour."

"I don't want to go home with another heartache."

He stared at her, a muscle working in his jaw, and she had no idea what ran through his thoughts. Finally, he nodded. "Very well, I'll move up hiring a new nanny. But right now, you're in my arms, in my bed, and I want you. I want you to stay. I want to kiss you all night," he said, trailing light kisses over her shoulder and scooting down.

Her heart drummed a frantic beat and she knew she couldn't deny him. She wanted to be with him.

He rolled over, holding his weight so he wasn't too heavy. She looked into his eyes and tingled. Desire blazed as if they hadn't just made love.

When his gaze lowered to her mouth, her heart pounded, and when he kissed her she moaned. *Don't fall in love with him. Don't play with fire.* The warnings echoed in her head, but they were too late.

She held him tightly, as if her arms were enough to keep her from having to face tomorrow and to soon say goodbye to him. But she knew that could never be. So instead, she simply let herself live the moment. She gave herself to him and opened up to him.

Later, when she finally started to get out of bed and move to her room, he pulled her back. "Amelia is asleep and no one else is coming in today. Stay with me and let me hold you."

This time there was no hesitation. "I can't say no to that request."

She would not move in with him, but she was with him every evening. They were becoming a family with little Amelia, and Erin was falling more in love with Cade each day. It wouldn't last, but she had made a choice and taken his advice about letting go and living. She wouldn't think about when she had to tell Cade and Amelia goodbye. That would come all too soon.

One night near the end of September when she was in Cade's arms after making love, she shifted and raised up to gaze into his eyes. "You said you would start interviewing for the new nanny in October. I think we should stick to that schedule. It's only a month earlier and it will make the adjustment for Amelia easier."

Cade wound long locks of her hair around his fingers as he met her gaze. "You're sure that's what you want? This is paradise, Erin."

"I think so, too, but I don't want to leave my heart behind, Cade. I've had enough heartbreak."

A muscle worked in his jaw as he stared at her in silence. "I don't want to hurt you," he said gruffly. "This has been the best, darlin'." Desire flared in the depths of his eyes and his arm slipped around her shoulders as he pulled her to him to kiss her. She wound her arms around him and kissed him in return, refusing to think about parting with him. It was too late to avoid being hurt, but she wasn't going to tell him.

He rolled her over, shifting over her as he plunged into her, and drove thoughts of tomorrow away.

In early October the new nanny interviews started as Cade had said they would. He interviewed each woman and narrowed down the pack to those he thought would be likely candidates as Amelia's new nanny. The next step was to let Erin interview them.

He had four women for her to interview and he listed them in order of his preference. At breakfast when he started to give her the rundown, she shook her head. "You keep your preferences to yourself, and after I interview them I'll make my own list and then we'll compare them. I don't want to be influenced by your choices."

"Fine. We'll do it however you want."

"It's nice you have all this faith in my selection. I'll be long gone."

"You love Amelia and you'll select the best one for her. I know that."

Erin stared at him and his dark brows arched in question. "What? Food on my face? Something I said? What's wrong?"

"It's something you said," she answered. "You said I love Amelia."

"But you do."

She nodded. "I do." She tried not to, but it had been a losing battle.

His blue eyes narrowed and he stared at her. "You knew when you took the job this might be a problem, but you'll get past it. That's just part of letting go and we have to—you know that."

"I thought maybe I could do this without it being so difficult to tell her goodbye," she said, knowing it was going to hurt a lot to say goodbye to Amelia and Cade.

"You definitely can stay and be her nanny until she's grown," he said, smiling at her.

"Thank you for that wonderful offer," she said, shaking her head and laughing with him even though she didn't feel like laughing. She had some tough times ahead when she had to leave them for good. It was going to hurt badly, but he was right. She had known it from the start.

He stood up and crossed the room to her to place his hands on her shoulders. "We're going to be right here on the ranch. Come back anytime you want to see her and stay as long as you want. I hope you and I don't have to say goodbye, either. I have a plane and I can fly to Austin to pick you up at school and fly you back here. We're not saying goodbye forever. I've been seeing you since you were six years old or younger. That won't end when you walk out the door."

Smiling, she nodded, thinking what it would be like if all that he said was the way it turned out to be. She knew when she walked out the door, it would be the end. Cade would go on with his life and someone else would be his latest interest and Amelia would have a new nanny to love, a more permanent nanny hopefully, and both Amelia and Cade would disappear from her life.

She would hear about them from her brother, but that would be seldom and probably even less now that he was out of the country.

The first few months after leaving Cade and Amelia were going to be the ones that would hurt the most. She'd just have to find a way to get through them and forget about the man and baby she'd fallen in love with. And she was in love with them. Both of them. She couldn't be intimate with Cade even for the short term without her heart being totally involved. But she hadn't told him, knowing they had no future.

She loved him, she just didn't know the depth of

her feelings for him and she hoped when she got away from him she would begin to get over him and he would become a memory. A memory so hot he had seared a permanent image in her brain.

Just as Adam had faded away and Cade had wiped out that hurt, she wondered if there would be someone to make her forget Cade.

But as her lips met his for a kiss, she already knew the answer to that question.

While Maisie watched Amelia, Erin interviewed the four women Cade had selected, and when the interviews were done, she knocked on the open door and walked into Cade's office.

Leaning back in his chair, he sat with his booted feet propped on the desk. His long jeans-clad legs were crossed and his blue denim shirt sleeves were rolled back. He finished his phone call, swung his feet to the floor and stood.

"Have a seat," he said, his gaze sweeping over her hair that was twisted and pinned behind her head. Looking professional, she wore a tailored brown suit with a tan silk blouse that had a V-shaped neckline and matching tan high-heeled pumps.

"I'm finished with the interviews," she said, handing him her list of candidates in the order in which she liked them.

His eyes scanned the names and he nodded. "We agree on the number one and number two choices, I see."

"Good. I'm glad we agreed on that. I thought our

first choice was the perfect candidate. She was very nice and has experience and a sweet manner. And she's a grandmother. They all live in Fort Worth or near there, so that would be a plus."

"Don't sound so eager."

She smiled at him, a bittersweet one. "The time will come when I move on."

He sat back, and she couldn't read the expression that overtook his face. "I've been making plans. I've already talked to Maisie and I've hired her to stay on the weekends for the first two months after you've gone and have Monday and Tuesday off instead. She'll cover the weekends and I'll be here during the week. If I have to travel, Maisie said she would work it out to stay and get someone to temporarily cook for her. How's that sound?"

"As if you've covered all the bases." So why did she feel as if someone had stuck a knife in her chest? The pain only got worse when she realized something. "I won't be here for Amelia's first birthday in January," she said. "I know it's a lot to dare hope you'll send me pictures."

"You could come home for it."

She shook her head. "When I'm gone, Cade. I won't be back," she said. The pain intensified and because she refused to show it to him, she had to get away. "Speaking of Maisie, I should get Amelia from her now, although I think I'll change clothes to something more casual before I take charge of Amelia." When she stood, he came to his feet to circle his desk and walk to her.

"You look gorgeous," he said. His voice had lowered and had a husky note, and she tingled from the desire in his expression. Reaching out, he wrapped his arms around her waist, leaned close and kissed her.

Surprised, she stood for just an instant and then wrapped her arms around his neck to kiss him in return. When he finally released her, she looked up at him. "What was that about?"

"It was because I know I'm going to have to tell you goodbye soon." He dropped another kiss to her lips. "Stay and talk to me after dinner tonight."

"I will, but that isn't really what you're asking me to do," she said, and he smiled at her as he draped his hand on her shoulder and caressed her nape with light strokes that sent tingles dancing down her spine.

"Cade," she whispered, looking up at him. He tightened his arm around her waist, hauling her against him, and leaned down to kiss her, a long, hungry kiss that made her think of lovemaking and long nights together. Finally she stepped back.

"I really need to get Amelia and give Maisie some relief."

"I'll get Amelia. But promise me that you'll sit with me tonight and not go flying off and shut yourself in your suite."

"You have a way of persuading me to do what you want," she said, smiling at him.

"Just sometimes and only when you want to."

"I'll see you at dinner."

"And I'll bring Amelia," he said, watching her

walk away. She glanced back over her shoulder at him to see him still standing there, his gaze sweeping every inch of her.

Lara Prentiss started the first of November. Cade had his men help her move and she temporarily took the suite across the hall from Amelia's. When Erin moved out, Lara would move into her suite.

Erin introduced the older woman to Amelia, watching Lara take Amelia and sit in the rocker to talk to her. Short, with graying hair and big blue eyes, Lara looked like Amelia's grandmother and Amelia seemed to like her from the first.

Erin hurt inside. She was losing another little baby in her life. Amelia wasn't her baby, but she loved her deeply and it was going to hurt to tell her goodbye. She had known this day would come and she had no misgivings for taking the job and she would never be sorry about her time with Amelia. She wondered whether she would ever regret being with Cade. Right now, she couldn't regret that, either.

During the day, there were more moments when Lara took Amelia and Erin had to step back and watch and let the older woman hold Amelia and talk to her and dress her.

In those moments she worked on finalizing her arrangements for school and preparing to move. Though she still managed to spend parts of the days and evenings with Amelia, she no longer saw as much of Cade and there were few evenings alone with him or nights with him until her last weekend in December.

Saturday night she was in Cade's arms in his big bed, after they'd made love, and he held her close against him. "What weekend would be good for me to fly to Austin to see you?"

Apparently what she'd told him hadn't sunk in, or he was still resisting. She looked up at him. "Cade, it's like I told you. When we tell each other goodbye here, that might as well be it."

He shifted slightly. "There's no need to cut off seeing each other."

"There's a big need," she said, running her hand over his muscled arm. "Neither of us is serious. Do you want to get married?"

He looked startled. "No. You know I'm not going to marry," he answered, frowning slightly. "That hasn't changed, Erin. I'm just not a marrying man and you know why."

"But I want marriage and children, and if I'm with you, I'll fall in love and want marriage eventually and you won't, so I think to avoid more heartache than I already have, we're breaking it off when I leave here. It's in my best interest. I hope to avoid getting hurt badly again. It's going to be hard enough to leave you and Amelia. I don't want to increase the pain and the longing."

"Well, hell, I don't want to do that, either. I didn't exactly have hurting you in mind. I want to kiss and hold you."

"Ultimately, if we do that, I'll have to know that I can count on those kisses and that love forever and you're not going to promise that or ever want it."

He shook his head. "I'm sorry, Erin, but you've known that from the first," he said, his dark eyes stormy as his thoughts raged. Then, finally, they settled. "All right. I don't want your brother to come home and find you crying over leaving here."

"I promise you he won't. As amazing as it is, I think I may be able to forget you," she teased while deep down, she knew she never would forget him.

He didn't smile, startling her. "Your brother will figure things out no matter what you do. He's always had a knack for coming to the right conclusion."

"Don't worry about Luke. He's at the South Pole and he won't be home until this is history."

"I'm going to miss you," Cade said solemnly. "Come back for Christmas with us. It'll be hell knowing Amelia doesn't have Nate and Lydia. Add to that going through the holidays without you. Come for a few days."

She shook her head. "Sorry, Cade. I'll be wound up in my family and I can't keep going through goodbyes." She wanted to say yes, wanted to be with them, but she couldn't take that emotional upheaval of another big goodbye. "Amelia will have a fun Christmas and she is too little to know what she's lost."

But Erin wasn't. She'd know every moment she'd lost with Cade and his baby.

When her last day arrived, Erin took Amelia to her suite to tell her goodbye. How would she ever get through saying goodbye and driving away without crying? She sat rocking and talking to Amelia who gazed at her with big blue eyes. Amelia had a new teddy bear from Erin and she was pulling on its eyes and ears.

"You're so sweet. I'll miss you every day and I know you're going to grow so fast that I won't recognize you when I see your pictures. I love you, Amelia. You be a sweet girl and good to your uncle Cade who will be a great daddy for you."

"Da-da," she said, looking at Erin.

"That's right. He's going to be a second daddy and you just call him da-da. He's going to take good care of you and love you to pieces. I'll come back to see you." She pulled Amelia close in her arms, letting tears spill down her cheeks. She stayed that way until Amelia pulled away slightly and settled against her. Erin brushed away her tears, trying to stop thinking about leaving, about missing Amelia and missing Cade. When she had her emotions under control, she stood.

"I think you're ready to go to sleep. I'm going to put you down. When you wake up, Lara will get you."

The door opened and she put her finger over her lips when Cade thrust his head into the room. She carried Amelia to her crib and placed her in it, then turned to tiptoe out.

Cade took her hand and went through the adjoining door into his suite. In his bedroom he turned to wrap his arms around Erin. He leaned forward to kiss her and paused, looking intently at her. He ran his thumb across her cheek.

"I'm going to miss her," she said, feeling tears

threaten again. She closed her eyes and he drew her close against him.

"You can come see her anytime you want."

She held him tightly, unable to speak past the lump in her throat.

Finally he walked out with her. Lara told her goodbye inside the house with Maisie and Harold, and Cade was the only one who walked her out to the car.

"If you'll go out with me, I'll fly to Austin next Saturday night."

"Thanks, but no. I'll just be getting settled in my new apartment. No telling what I'll be busy doing." She opened the car door, then turned back around. "Send me a picture of Amelia occasionally."

He smiled. "I'll do that and I'll plan for a visit in the near future."

"Call first. Otherwise, I might be buried in my studies."

"Sure," he said, gazing intently at her. "You're not going to let me come see you, are you?"

"I don't see that as being good for either one of us. I'll think it over."

He put his hand behind her head, held here there for a long, passionate kiss. When he released her and stepped back, she was breathing hard.

"On that note, I better go," she said. "Goodbye, Cade. Thanks for hiring me as your nanny."

"See you, Erin," he said, staring intently at her.

She got in the car and drove away and to her relief, tears didn't start until she was around the first curve that hid his house from view. After a few min-

utes the tears flowed so freely she had to pull over.
She didn't know whether she was crying more over
telling Amelia goodbye or telling Cade. She loved the
little girl and had many recent pictures of her on her
phone, but they would get old. Amelia would grow
and this time would be a memory.

And what about Cade? She could see him, and
she'd end up sleeping with him, but that would only
lead to more hurt. At some point he would tire of seeing her and break it off, or he'd get involved with another woman, one who was available to him. And the
pain would just get worse. No, she was doing the right
thing. Now had to be the time to end any relationship.

If she'd learned anything in the past few years, it
was this. Love hurt. She pulled the car back onto the
road and headed to Austin, determined to not get en-
tangled in any relationship. Her heart was still broken from this one.

Erin moved through her tiny Austin apartment getting it ready for when she started school the first week
of January. Missing Amelia and Cade more than ever,
she constantly took out her phone, started to send a
text to Cade and then put away her phone, knowing
she had to sever the ties.

When she first moved to Austin, Cade had called
a few times and they had talked for over an hour each
time as he'd filled her in about Amelia, but now she
usually let his calls go unanswered. It was for the
best, she told herself.

Tears spilled down Erin's cheeks and she wiped

them away. She missed them both more than she had thought she would. When she saw little girls in strollers or dads carrying their little girls, she had to fight back tears.

Even the holidays had been difficult. She had returned home but of course Luke hadn't been there. Though she and her family had talked to him on Christmas, it hadn't been the same as having her brother beside her. And she couldn't stop thinking of the other people she was missing. Cade and Amelia celebrating the day without her.

One of the days at home her mother came into the utility room while Erin was sorting her laundry to pack. "Are you all right, Erin? You don't look like you are."

"I'm fine, Mom."

Her mother stepped close to put her arm around her. "You miss that little girl, don't you?"

Tears filled Erin's eyes and she wiped them away. "I miss her more than I thought I would," she said. "But when I get in school, I'll get over missing her and life will get busy and go on and I'll be okay. Don't you worry. School should take my mind off her."

"Erin, is it just Amelia? It isn't Cade, too, is it?"

She turned to look at her mother and she couldn't tell her anything except the truth. "I miss him, but we didn't have any future together. He's a bachelor. You should know because he and Luke were so close."

"Luke was a little worried when he talked to Cade about hiring you. I really thought you'd be all right."

"I am. I promise. Don't worry about me."

"Well, I know you'll get busy with school, but I hate to see you hurt and I know you're hurting over leaving them."

"I couldn't stay. Cade and I are not good for each other and I can't hang around because of Amelia."

"If you miss Amelia and Cade, go see them."

"I'll think about that, Mom."

Her mother hugged her. "I better check on dinner. Take care of yourself."

"Thanks. I will," she said, thinking the best way to take care of herself was to avoid seeing Cade or Amelia because she would have to go through another goodbye. And her heart couldn't take that.

After New Year's Day, she drove back to Austin. The first week of January her classes started and it was a relief to be so busy, she didn't have time for her mind to wander to life on Cade's ranch.

Who was she kidding? Her mind was never far from there. Amelia would adjust because children did, but did Cade miss her? Was he already seeing someone else? How deep had his feelings run?

Eight

Cade rocked Amelia, who was sprawled against him, one small arm over her head as she slept quietly. He could put her in her crib, but he continued rocking her. He remembered seeing Erin rocking her, a low lamp shining soft light over her.

He missed her more than he thought possible. He knew he would miss her at first, but he expected that to pass, so this constant thinking about Erin, wanting to be with her, wanting to talk to her, surprised him. Missing her not only hadn't diminished, it had gotten worse. He thought he missed her more now than when she'd left in December.

He'd had relationships that had meant something to him and when they had broken up, he had been able to move on. He'd expected that to happen this time, too, because he'd never had anything lasting with Erin. It was brief and then she was gone. And aside from a few phone calls they hadn't kept in touch, which was Erin's doing. She didn't seem to want to keep up with each other or even see each other again. He could fly to Austin, but she hadn't indicated that she wanted him to do so.

It was difficult to concentrate on the ranch and at times during the day he would find his thoughts wandering back to her and he'd forget what he was doing.

He looked down at Amelia who snuggled against him. He still hurt over the loss of Nathan and Lydia and he hurt for Amelia, but he was determined to be the best possible substitute dad for her. He wanted to shield her from hurt.

His thoughts jumped back to Erin. Had she started dating? She wanted marriage and she was gorgeous, so probably she had been asked out. The thought of her kissing another guy, let alone getting married, bothered him. One more shocking turn in his life. He had never felt that way about a woman before. In the past when he'd had an affair, once they had parted, he had never cared what the woman did. Actually, he usually remained friends with them and wished them well.

That was not the case when he thought about Erin.

Amelia stirred and he carefully patted her and sung softly. It was the weekend and Lara had gone to Dallas until Sunday night. He no longer worried about caring for Amelia. He was comfortable with her, sure of himself, and he had fun taking care of her. Too many times he wished Erin was with him to laugh at Amelia's antics or to share a moment.

He sat in the rocker singing softly to her and patting her back lightly. He brushed curls away from her face and realized he loved her as much as he would have if she had been his baby.

"Good night, sweet girl. I'll hear you if you need me," he said, finally placing her in her crib and going to his bedroom, leaving the door open between them.

He took out his cell phone and called Erin. "Answer, Erin," he whispered, wishing she would pick up her phone and wondering where she was and what she was doing. He missed her, and the house was big and empty and Amelia was asleep. He felt restless, dissatisfied, wishing he could talk to Erin. Had she seen that he called and deliberately wasn't taking his call or was she just busy doing something else? Was she out with someone?

That question was torment and he tried to think about other things. But his mind was traveling a single track. He missed Erin and he wanted to see her. He couldn't even get her to answer her phone when he called, so he was certain if he flew to Austin, she wouldn't go out to dinner with him. She wouldn't go out with him when she had been here and he had asked her.

He swore under his breath and stared at his phone, finally sending her a text. There was no answer, so he put away his phone. He couldn't be in love because that wasn't even on his horizon. It was no part of his life. He'd never had a broken heart and he wasn't suffering one now. He just missed her being with him.

A week later he stood on his porch as Blake drove up in his pickup and climbed out, crossing the backyard to the porch. "This is nice of you to let us have Amelia's baby things that she no longer uses, the little basket and the carrier, all the baby blankets. Sierra is due any day now, so she told me to get everything so we can have it ready."

"When are you going back to your house in Dallas?"

"Tonight. Her doctor is in Dallas instead of Downly and that's a bigger hospital. Sierra is there now and we'll stay in Dallas until our baby is born. It's so exciting. I love that we're having a girl because she and Amelia should be close."

"Come on and I'll help you carry everything to your truck. It's all in the storage room."

"What do you hear from Erin Dorsey?" Blake asked as he followed his brother.

"Not much. We don't talk."

Blake stared at him. "Did you part on good terms?"

"Sure. She's just busy with school and we've gone our separate ways."

"How does her brother like the South Pole?"

"That's Luke's deal—he loves it. He'll be at a research center for a year. Glad it's him and not me." Cade opened the door off the utility room to a large storage space with windows on two sides and shelves lining all the walls. "Here's the bassinet and a little tub. All these things go. There's two umbrella strollers because we had three of them. These are extras that we had that were presents." He picked up a toy and held it in his hands, remembering Erin using it to play with Amelia when she first came and making Amelia laugh.

"Cade?"

Startled, he looked around, momentarily dazed, forgetting he had been helping Blake get baby things. "Sorry, I was thinking about when I first got Amelia," he said.

"Sure," Blake said, staring at him and then lifting a box. "Does this go? It has 'Blake' written on it."

Cade looked at it and opened the lid. "Erin marked this for you and Sierra because it's baby things that Amelia has outgrown."

"How's the new nanny working out?"

"Fine. Lara's good and Amelia seems happy with her."

"At least Erin was here to get her started. I wish we had a chance to hire Erin for the first year, but I don't expect she'll be interested in another nanny job."

"She wasn't interested in this one. I paid her extra to get her to take it," Cade said, looking into another box. As he raised the lid a piece of paper fluttered out. Cade picked it up and looked at a selfie he had taken. Him with Amelia and Erin. He was holding Amelia and had the arm holding the camera around Erin and they were leaning close together. He stared at it now, looking at Erin and missing her, wishing she were here.

"Hey, Cade." Blake's interruption made him look

up. "What about this?" He was standing there, holding another box.

Cade shook his head and his brother looked amused as he stepped closer to look at the picture he was obviously so engrossed in. "Good selfie."

Cade smiled. "Sorry. I was thinking about when we took this picture."

"Sure you haven't talked to her recently?"

"No, I haven't. She worked for me and she's gone."

"Maybe you ought to give her a call." He looked down at the stack of baby items they'd amassed. "I'll take all this stuff now and come back and get the rest later," Blake said. But he paused before he bent down to pick up the boxes. "I suppose she knows how opposed you are to marriage."

"Oh, sure. I'll get the rest of this." Cade picked up another carrier and an infant car seat.

They worked in silence to load the pickup and finally Cade jumped down as Blake came around the front of the pickup. "We sure thank you for all this."

"I don't need it now. You wouldn't think one little baby would have so much that a pickup can't hold it all," he said, glancing at the overstuffed truck. "But Erin knew what she had outgrown." As he mentioned her name, he couldn't help thinking of her again.

Blake pushed his hat to the back of his head and wiped his brow. "You know, since you were old enough to think about it, you swore you would never get married. You may not even know it when you fall in love."

Cade turned to stare at Blake. "Run that by me again."

"You heard me. It's sort of like I was about our father. I was so busy being angry all the years I was growing up that when I started in business, I still thought of him as a big, powerful man. I wanted to compete with him and beat him because when I became an adult, I thought I could. I never factored in that he would get old and weak. I actually felt sorry for him when we finally got together."

"That's hard to figure. You have lots of reasons to dislike him."

"Well, I don't feel the way I did anymore. Maybe you're unrealistic in your views that you shouldn't marry. Our dad is not an example of how the whole world is. He's a frail old man now and I didn't get a shred of satisfaction out of ruining his hotel business. I just didn't look at it closely enough and maybe you aren't, either. Maybe you can't even recognize if you're in love because you've got that warped view of marriage."

"Thank you, Doctor. I'll think about your advice."

"I still say, maybe you ought to try again to get in touch with Erin. You're not quite yourself."

Cade stared at him. "And you're loco. I just think back when I was a kid and how lousy home life was sometimes. I don't want to be tied down and find myself in that kind of situation."

"Maybe you need to see a doctor, then. You're not yourself."

"You wait until your baby arrives and then I can

tell you that you're not yourself. Just wait until you're taking care of a little one and see if you don't change. They get you up in the middle of the night and they can't tell you why they're crying. You don't know what they want, or if they hurt—that's new in my life."

Blake shook his head. "Maybe that's it. Time will tell. Thanks again for the baby things."

"Sure. Glad you have them now. Let us know when this little girl arrives."

"You'll know," Blake said. He turned to get into the pickup, then stopped and turned back. "Cade, I hope to hell you and I are both better dads than the one we had."

"I was afraid of that, but now that I'm a dad to Amelia I'm not going to be like our dad. And neither are you. I can't wait to come home to Amelia after I've been out working all day. I think she's awesome. I'll always tell her about Nate, but I feel like her dad, too."

"You *are* her dad, too. And I know you're a good one. And I know you're right that we'll never be like our dad," he said. "Thank goodness." He got into the truck, and then looked out the rolled-down window at Cade. "Better go try to call Erin again," he said, looking amused. "You might be getting back what you've been giving out."

As Blake drove down the road to the highway, Cade walked back to the house, thinking about what his brother had said. Was he in love with Erin and didn't even know it because he had never been in love before?

That night Cade sat in his office, papers shoved aside as he held Erin's picture and wondered about her feelings and about his own.

She had urged him to marry, telling him that he wouldn't be like his father. For the first time in his life, he realized she was right. He'd told Blake as much that afternoon. His parents had fought so much, yet before they married they were in love and that was what had always scared him—people who were in love reaching a point where they were so estranged they were angry with each other anytime they were together.

Maybe it didn't have to get that way.

Erin's parents weren't that way. They had been happily married for over twenty-five years. Maybe his views of himself and marriage were misguided. He had once told Erin to let go and live—maybe he was the one who should rethink long-held beliefs that held him back.

The thought startled him because all his life, as far back as he could recall, he had determined that he would never marry. Could he change that thinking?

A far more important question—was he in love with Erin?

He didn't know anything about falling in love. All he knew was that he wanted her with him. He wanted to hold her, kiss her and love her. He missed her, and he missed her all through the day, not only at night. He missed her laughter, her way with Amelia, her outlook, her jokes. He missed the way he felt when he was with her. Was that love?

Would he want to be married, to live with her for the rest of his life? Would he want her in his bed every night? That question set him on fire and the answer was a no-brainer. Maybe Blake had been right—maybe he was in love with her. So what now? Did he want to propose? Would she be leery about his turnaround and find it difficult to believe that he really was in love and wanted to marry her?

He could easily imagine Erin doubting that he knew what he was doing when it came to proposing marriage. Could he convince her that he meant it with all his heart? That he wasn't like her ex-fiancé and he wanted her for life?

The thought stopped him cold. It was all true. He loved Erin and he wanted to marry her. He had to make her believe him.

He tried to call her again and got no answer. Cade jammed his hands into his pockets and paced the room. If she wouldn't take his calls, how could he tell her he loved her?

Erin's cell phone buzzed and she looked up from her notebook to grab her phone to see if she had a text from her family. Startled, she saw it was from Luke.

Quickly scanning his brief text she saw he would be in Dallas for meetings later in the week. While he was in the US, he planned to fly to Austin and take her to dinner.

She hurried to a mirror to look at her image. She

didn't want Luke to know that she was in love with
Cade. Luke would be furious with Cade if he thought
Cade had caused her the least bit of hurt. And her
brother would blame Cade completely. He would
think Cade seduced her and planned on seduction
from the first and that she hadn't been able to defend
herself from his charm because she was so vulnerable
over her broken engagement. He would be so angry
with Cade, he would end the friendship and if he saw
Cade, he would probably punch him.

She couldn't tell Luke not to come. First of all,
she wanted to see him. Second, if she told him not
to come, he would know there was a reason and he
would come see her. She wrote back that she would
be happy to have dinner with him and she couldn't
wait to see him. She would just wear something that
made her look good and try to be so cheerful that
he wouldn't guess that she had been unhappy at all.

Friday night she opened the door to face her
brother, who gave her a big hug and then smiled.
"It's good to see you. How's the student?"

"Isn't this wonderful? I love it here. You look great.
I like your haircut," she said, looking at his thick,
short, blond hair that still curled over his head. "I'm
so glad you're home and you flew here to see me.
While I get my things, come look at my apartment."

Luke stepped inside, but he was clearly more interested in talking than touring her place. "Austin is
beautiful," he said. "After the frozen ice cap, I'm in
paradise."

"It's still winter, Luke. Come back in the spring

and it'll be gorgeous. The bluebonnets will be in bloom and Texas really will be paradise."

"How was the job with Cade?"

"Great and Amelia is the sweetest little baby you ever saw."

"Nate was a great guy. He was younger so I didn't know him like I did Cade. I know little brother Gabe well enough to know he asked you out."

She smiled again. "Yes, he did and no, I didn't go out with him, but he was cheerful and friendly and Amelia liked him."

"Sure. Everyone likes Gabe. He's always got a grin and he loves the pretty ladies, but I figured you'd brush him off. He isn't any more serious about women than Cade, though. Their father really messed up those boys."

"I hope not permanently."

"I think Blake made peace with the old man. You hear from Cade?"'

The question was casual, but she knew Luke was paying attention. "No," was all she said, and she hoped that was all Luke would want to know or say about Cade.

"Enough about the Callahans. Mom and Dad said to give you a hug for them. Everything is about the same at home and it was good to be there and eat Mom's beef stew again."

"Don't even talk about it," she joked as she touched her belly and rolled her eyes. "I miss it already. But I do have a good restaurant picked out for tonight. You said not to worry about expense."

"I meant it. I know what it's like to be in college. Always hungry and always broke."

She laughed. "I think that fits the male population more than the female."

They went to an elegant steak house and Luke insisted she order a steak. She couldn't imagine how she would get through even a quarter of the steak, but it would give her leftovers for a few nights.

As they ate, she listened as he described aspects of his environmental engineering job and a new million-dollar wastewater treatment plant and the success in dealing with gray water. She could tell he loved his work and loved the Antarctic.

"Erin, I wish you could see Antarctica. The ice and snow are beautiful. The air isn't polluted and you can see tiny details so much farther away than you can here. It's amazing."

While he talked about a conference in São Paulo and his traveling to Torres del Paine when he had some time off, Erin tried to be filled with cheer. After all, they were on to safe topics now. Or so she thought, until Luke's next question.

"Who did you date while you worked for Cade? I know Cade and I know he won't ever leave things at the status quo. I'm sure he tried to introduce you to someone."

She swallowed her steak. "Actually, no, he didn't. Maybe he's changed. With the responsibility for Amelia, he stuck very close to home."

"Who's he dating?"

She shrugged. "He wasn't. I think he was so worried about Amelia, he gave up other activities. He was scared to pieces to take care of her."

"That doesn't sound like the Cade I know except for being scared to pieces over his charge," Luke remarked drily. "You didn't go out with anyone and he didn't go out with anyone?"

"That's right. Luke, it's a ranch out in the boonies. We had a baby to take care of, so we concentrated on her. Cade's grandmother was worn-out and couldn't cope when I arrived. Then he hired the next nanny earlier than he had planned originally. That was good because it gave her more time while I was there to get used to Amelia and vice versa."

"Ah, he hired the new nanny early," he repeated, sounding pleased. Luke talked some more about the station where he was, the storms they'd had, the incredible temperatures and the weather. He looked robust, fit and filled with energy.

"Erin, you're not eating anything."

Since he'd brought up Cade and dating, she'd put her fork down. "I had a big lunch today and I'm just not hungry."

He stared at her. "You look really thin."

"It's all the walking I'm doing," she said, getting worried because her brother knew her well.

"How many miles do you walk a day?"

"Luke, stop quizzing me."

"Do you have pictures of Amelia?"

"Yes," she said, relieved to show him the pictures. "I have some here on my phone and I have some more really cute ones on my iPad at home. When we go

back, I'll show them to you." As she scrolled through
the pictures of Amelia smiling into the camera, she
felt the familiar pangs in her heart.

"She's a cute little kid and I can imagine that
Cade was worried about taking care of her because
he doesn't know one thing about little kids."

"She's really easy to care for," Erin said, knowing Amelia would be in bed asleep now. What would
Cade be doing?

"I'm not sure I did you any favors by recom-
mending you to Cade," Luke said quietly, and she
looked up at him.

"You really love her, don't you?" he asked.

"Maybe I do, but that's all right. I can go see her
whenever I want to and Maisie can keep me posted
about her."

"Maisie—I hadn't thought about her. Was she
around much?"

"She was there all the time. She would stay on
weekends if Cade asked her and she would fill in if
needed, although I didn't go anywhere. Maisie helped
constantly."

"Did Cade take you out?"

She smiled. "No, Cade did not take me out," she
said, thankful again she had turned down his invitation.

"That kind of surprises me."

"I told you, we were busy with Amelia. You try
taking care of a baby and see how much spare time
you have. I'm a good nanny."

"I know that."

After that, his questions stopped and he signaled the waiter for the check. When he'd paid, he said, "Let's go back so I can get a good look at your apartment."

After she'd given him the tour they sat in her small front room and Luke sipped a cold beer while she drank ice water.

"Where are the pictures of Amelia you said you'd show me? I got you into that job and I'd like to know that it worked out well and you were happy."

"Didn't I look happy in the pictures that were on my phone?"

"Yes, you looked very happy. Happier than you do now."

"You're imagining things," she said. "Maybe I should quiz you and see if you're really happy in the frozen south because that sounds miserably cold."

"It is miserably cold, but I like the work. It's what I wanted to do and I'm learning a lot, using my education some. I like what I do."

"Well, good. I'll get you another beer."

"I'll get it," he said, getting up. "Stay where you are. Want anything?"

"No, thanks. I'm fine." He left the room and she sipped her water. A few minutes later he returned with pictures in his hands.

"I saw these in the kitchen. You printed them out."

"Yes. Sit on the sofa and I'll look at them with you," she said, wishing she had taken out the one of Cade with her. She guessed Luke would make an issue of it.

She sat close beside him as he looked through them. When he took a draft of his beer she said, "That's your last beer because you're driving."

"Sure, Mom. I'll drink a big glass of water before I leave. That'll help."

"Yes, it will. I'll go get you one."

"You stay where you are. I'm not going to drink water with my beer. I'll get it soon." He flipped to the next photo. "Ahh, she's a cute little girl. That wreck of Nate's really tore Cade up and I can understand. It seemed so senseless and tragic."

The next picture was the one of her and Cade. She stood beside him and he had his arm around her shoulders, his face close to hers and they were both laughing.

Luke stared at it and then looked at her. She saw the realization and accusation in his eyes before he spoke. "This is why you're so thin and you look like you're going to burst into tears."

"I miss them and I miss Amelia and I'm going to burst into tears if you don't stop."

"Dammit. I debated telling him about you and urging him to hire you, but there were so many reasons I thought he'd leave you alone."

"Will you listen?" she said. "You're going to upset me and that I don't need. Cade and I don't communicate and don't intend to in the future. I told him and Amelia goodbye. They're out of my life."

"Yet you have these pictures you went to the trouble to print. Especially this one." He held up the photo of her and Cade. "Dammit, I told him all you had gone through."

"Stop getting angrier at him. He didn't do anything and we've parted forever. I'm in school and I made a lot of money working for him. I loved being a nanny and I loved little Amelia. Now promise me you'll leave him alone."

"Hell, no, I'm not leaving him alone." Luke caught her chin in his hand. "You're in love with him, aren't you?" he said, his blue eyes boring into her. "You are."

"You're being a bossy big brother. I'll get over Cade and you forget this," she snapped, jerking her chin out of his hand and taking her pictures from him. She crossed the room to sit and glare at him.

"Now, you're not going to do anything foolish, are you?" she asked.

"No, I'm not. I don't have time for Cade and I hope you meet some nice guy getting his PhD, date him and marry him."

She had to laugh. "Stop trying to marry me off. You've been in the frozen south too long. You need to get back with your penguins." Luke grinned and she wondered if he really had lost his anger. "You leave Cade alone. I'm fine and I don't want him around. Okay?"

"Okay. You know what you want, but if he tries to hire you back or anything else, then he'll hear from me when I get back in the USA."

"Luke, promise me you won't do anything rash.

I'm fine. I won't take his calls because I see no point in it."

Luke turned his head. "You don't take his calls?"

"No. Didn't you just hear what I said? I don't take Cade's calls. We're through. I'm enrolled in school. I'm halfway across Texas from him. He's out of my life for good. What more could you want? Now if you go punch him, then I'll have to go see about him. Is that what you want?"

"Hell, no," he said. "Okay, you made your point and I'll forget Cade, but he didn't do what I asked and I'm sorry if I sent you somewhere that caused you more trouble."

"Forget it. I got the job, got paid way more than it was worth. I did get to take care of little Amelia who is a sweetheart. I miss her, but that's natural. Cade is out of my life forever," she said, feeling something squeeze inside. "What more could you want?"

"I guess not anything. That's good." Luke stood. "Sis, I better head back. I don't want the plane to go to Dallas without me."

"Thanks for coming out to see me. Bossy as you are, I wish you could stay just one night."

"I'd like to, but I haven't spent enough time with our folks. I'll go home and do that and then be on my way back to the Polar Regions."

She hugged him. "You're a good brother, Luke."

"I'm a super brother," he corrected her and then chuckled, and she punched his upper arm playfully as they walked to the door. He hugged her lightly.

"Take care of yourself and stay away from Cade. He won't ever get serious."

"I know," she said, "and I want marriage and a family."

"That's because our family is a good one and we all love each other." He kissed her cheek.

"Be careful, Luke," she said. She worried about him going back to the Antarctic. They argued, but he was her brother and she loved him and looked up to him and wanted him to be safe.

"I'll be careful and I'll be in Texas for a few more days."

She watched him drive away and then she rushed to phone Cade. She paused with her hand on her phone. "Just call him and tell him about Luke and get off the phone," she whispered to herself. "Don't talk to him for an hour," she added, knowing she would be tempted.

But could she do it? She stood there arguing with herself about calling him. Several times she put down her phone and walked away and then stopped and re-thought what she should do. Finally, taking a deep breath, she pressed his number.

The moment she heard his deep voice, tingles raced over her nerves and her pulse beat faster. Silently, she reminded herself to avoid letting him know how much she missed him.

"Cade, this is Erin. Listen to me," she blurted out. "My brother is home for a week and he flew here to have dinner with me. He's on his way back home to

Downly. I think he's really angry. Promise me you won't see him." She said it all in one breath and then she waited for his answer.

Nine

"Did you hear me?"

"I heard you and I'm not home and I won't see him," Cade said, and she let out her breath with relief.

"I'm sorry. He saw some pictures, those selfies you took and he got angry and started quizzing me."

"I'm far more interested in talking to you than hearing about Luke. I'm glad you called me. I've missed you."

Her heart thudded and she gripped the phone tightly. "I've missed you and Amelia so much," she admitted, tears coming because she just wanted to walk into Cade's strong arms and kiss him.

"Well, we can remedy some of that real soon."

She wiped her eyes. "How's that?" she asked, hoping he couldn't tell she was crying.

"Open your front door."

Shocked, she turned to stare at her door. She dropped her phone and ran to the door to open it. Cade stood on her porch and she felt as if she were in a dream. He had his black Stetson squarely on his head. He wore a leather Western jacket and jeans and boots and he looked more wonderful than he ever had before. She flung herself into his arms as he stepped into her house. He kissed her, walking her backward into the apartment and kicking the door closed behind him.

"Why are you here?" she whispered.

"Because I missed you and I love you," he answered, his blue eyes darker than ever. "And you wouldn't answer my calls, so I had to come in person."

"Cade," she gasped. "I've missed you so much."

"Then why in the hell didn't you take my calls? I've called and called," he said between light kisses.

"Because we don't have any future together," she said, tears welling again. He kissed her passionately, and she forgot about the future as she clung to him, kissing him, pouring all her longing into her kiss and pressing tightly against him. Her heart pounded with joy. For right now, he was here in her arms. She would worry about saying goodbye later.

Picking her up, he glanced around. "Bedroom?"

She pulled his head down to kiss him as she pointed over her shoulder. She held him tightly with one arm around his neck while her other hand roamed over him as if to make sure he was really there.

Cade carried her to her bed and set her on her feet while still kissing her. As her hands fluttered over him and she tugged off his shirt, unfastened and opened his belt, he pulled her sweater over her head and unfastened her jeans to push them away. He paused a moment to look at her, framing her face with his warm hands. "I've missed you like hell."

"I'm glad," she whispered, standing on tiptoe to kiss him. Her hands shook with eagerness and she continued kissing him. She couldn't believe he was here and she could kiss and hold him.

He picked her up, gazing into her eyes. "I love you, Erin," he said, and her heart thudded.

"I love you," she whispered in return, meaning it with all her heart. "More than anyone ever," she added and then kissed him.

Over an hour later she lay in Cade's arms, stroking his back while euphoria enveloped her. She wanted the night to last forever, to stay in his arms, to have his kisses, to be able to hold and love him.

"I love you so much," she whispered.

He shifted, placing her on the bed and rising up to look down at her. "I love you, Erin. And I mean this with all my heart and all my being—will you marry me?"

Erin's heart slammed against her ribs and she couldn't get her breath. Her arms tightened around his neck as she pulled him down to kiss him. Finally, she raised her head to look at him. "I love you, Cade. I love you and I'll always love you, but you've spent your life determined you would never marry. This isn't like you. Do you know what you're doing?"

"I'm more certain than I've ever been in my life. It was easy to say I didn't want to marry and never would want to, because I wasn't in love. Now I'm in love with you and I want to spend my life with you."

She framed his face with her hands. "I love you. You're a wonderful daddy for Amelia. You'll be a wonderful dad for all your children, Cade, but you have to be really sure. You may just want me in your bed and you're not accustomed to hearing no. Marriage is a giant change in your life."

He smiled at her and caressed her nape, making her tingle. "I'm really sure. It is a giant change I'm ready to make. Amelia was a revelation in my life—I can be a dad to her. That was a miracle to me. You've helped me see that I'm a good dad to her. You're right, Erin. I'm not like my father. I don't have to avoid marriage if I really love someone and now I do. I love you with all my heart."

Her heart pounded as she gazed at him and he looked at her, waiting without talking. "You mean that, don't you?" she asked. "And you're not scared I might not be able to have your biological children? We might have to adopt."

"Erin, I'm adopting Amelia. Why would I object to adopting another child?"

"Or children," she said, smiling at him. "I want a big family."

"And I want you. I'm not worried about your ability to have children. I think you can." He stopped her with a kiss when she started to deny his words. "I know—I'm an optimist. That's true, but love can do a lot in our lives. Whatever happens, we'll be together. Any kids we have, any way we have them, we'll love them. Darlin', I need you in my life. I've learned that during the past month. I love you," he whispered and kissed her hard and long.

She wanted him, loved him and wanted to yield to him, to toss cares and worries and common sense aside and tell him yes, she would marry him because she loved him and she loved Amelia and they would be a family. But she never got the chance. He rambled on, like a man who had a lot to say and he wasn't letting anything or anyone get in his way.

"I'm not scared to take a chance on being a husband or a dad. I've been miserable without you. I've thought about your career—you can still get your degree and you can work with children or human services or whatever you want. There will be needy families and children in Dallas, Fort Worth, Downly—you won't have any difficulty going on with your career if you want—part-time or full-time."

The more he spoke, the more her surprise grew. "You've thought about this a lot," she said, a small smile teasing her lips.

"I have thought about it and I put off Amelia's first birthday party because she's too little to know the difference. I wanted you there for it, so I waited."

Delighted, Erin hugged him as she kissed him again. "Thank you! I'm so glad. That will be fun. I love Amelia." She gazed up at him, looking into those dark blue eyes that she loved so much. "I love you with all my heart, but I'm stunned. How long have you thought about marriage?"

"Not a long time because I didn't realize I'd fallen in love. I've never really been in love before. Not the real thing—the forever kind of love." He kissed her and she held him tightly, kissing him in return while her heart pounded with joy.

She heard a car door slam, but paid little attention until she heard pounding on her door.

"What the hell?" Cade snapped, frowning.

She slipped out of bed and began yanking on clothes. "I just know that's Luke. He left, but somehow he must have found out you're here," she said. "I'll take care of him."

"You leave him to me," Cade said, passing her. He already had his jeans on and his feet jammed into his boots. He yanked on his shirt as he left the room. She buttoned her blouse and tucked it in, hurrying as fast as possible because she wanted to get the door and keep Luke and Cade apart.

"Cade, wait," she cried, running toward the front door to try reach it before he did. But she didn't make it.

Cade yanked open the door and Luke stepped forward. "Dammit, Cade. I told you not to hurt her," he snapped as he swung his fist and hit Cade, knocking him off his feet.

As Cade slammed against a chair and went down, Erin screamed and went to him.

"Cade," she said, cradling his cheeks in her hands

and turning his head toward her, afraid Luke had knocked him unconscious. Blood streamed from a cut on his cheekbone but he was alert. She looked into his eyes and all her anger with her brother evaporated. All she saw was the love and the desire she felt mirrored in Cade's gaze.

"Get up, dammit," Luke snapped.

She wrapped her arms around Cade's neck and hugged him. As long as she was over him, holding him, he wouldn't get up and her brother couldn't hit him. She gazed into his dark eyes.

"You never answered me," Cade said.

For a moment she thought he wasn't thinking straight, that her brother's punch had done more damage.

"This wasn't the way I imagined proposing to you," he went on to say, "but I can't wait. I love you. Will you marry me?"

"Get up, Cade," Luke ground out between clenched teeth. "Stop hiding behind Erin."

Cade ignored his friend's words. His eyes never wavered from hers. "Darlin', I love you."

"What the hell is going on?" Luke asked. "Get out of the way, Erin."

"Darlin', you still haven't answered my question. Will you marry me?" Cade asked.

"Yes," she gasped, giving up and wanting him and hoping she wasn't doing something that she would regret, but she couldn't say no. She loved him.

She kissed him, and then raised her head. "Cade, you're hurt—"

"I feel no pain." He grinned. "Because you'll marry me."

This time when Luke barked his command, Erin turned, scrambled up and faced her brother with her fists clenched.

"Don't you dare hit him again," she snapped. "I'm going to marry him. You hit him, Luke, and I don't know if I'll ever forgive you. You hit the man I'm going to marry. He's going to be your brother-in-law," she repeated louder as Cade came to his feet, wrapped his arm around her waist and lifted her out of his way while he faced Luke.

Luke's mouth dropped open as he stared from his sister to Cade.

"What the hell is going on? You're marrying my sister?"

"Yes, I am, as soon as I can."

"You owe him an apology and me an apology, Luke Dorsey," she said, getting between them again.

"Well, I'll be damned," Luke said, shaking his head. "Cade, I'm sorry."

Wiping his cheek with his handkerchief, Cade drew Erin into his arms to kiss her again. He held her tightly and finally raised his head to look into her eyes. "You'll really marry me?"

"Yes, I'll really marry you," she said, her heart pounding with joy as she clung to him to pull his head down to kiss him again. While they kissed, Cade reached behind him and closed the door.

"Where's Luke?" she asked, looking around.

"I don't know. I think he had the good sense to go."

Cade reached into his jeans pocket and pulled out a small box that he handed to her. "This is for you. I got this in case I could talk you into saying yes."

Her lips smiling and her hands shaking, she opened the box. She gasped when she saw a large diamond surrounded by dazzling emeralds.

"Cade, this is beautiful."

"So's my love," he said, drawing her to him to kiss her again. He picked her up and carried her to the bedroom to set her on her feet right beside the bed. She still held the ring and he took it from her to slip it onto her finger. "I need to ask your dad for your hand in marriage."

She laughed. "That's old-fashioned and I love it and he will probably be impressed because he asked my granddad. Some old customs still hang around in our family."

"How about kissing the bride-to-be and taking her to bed for a night of love?"

"I think that's perfect," she said, holding him tightly as if she might lose him again. "I might even drop out of school for you."

"Don't decide that tonight because I think you'll want to finish and get that degree," he said and kissed away her answer. "There are a lot of things you can do to help little kids when you have it."

She kissed Cade, joy chasing away all doubts and fears as she held him tightly and thought about Amelia. Erin's joy grew because she would get to be a real second mother for Amelia. She would be Cade's wife. She held him tightly, not wanting to ever let him go again.

Epilogue

On a sunny March morning Erin stood in the back room of the church while her mother smoothed the skirt of her white silk wedding dress that had narrow straps over her shoulders, a tiny waist and straight skirt. She wore the emerald and diamond necklace Cade had given her that matched her engagement ring and her hair was in spiral curls framing her face.

Erin held Amelia in her arms. Amelia had a pink hair bow in her dark curls and she wore a pink organdy dress.

"Mama," she said, playing with Erin's necklace.

"She calls me that and Cade dada," she told her own mother, unable to hide the pleasure in her voice. "When she's a little older, we'll tell her about her real mother and daddy. She already recognizes their pictures." They had two big paintings of them in their ranch house, among some family pictures, and a wonderful photo taken with Amelia the week before the crash that they'd framed and hung on the wall, too.

"That's good, honey," her mother said, smiling at Amelia. She took her from Erin and set her on her feet, holding her hand. "She's a strong little girl."

"She's a joy every day to me. Mom, I'm so happy."

Her mother moved close to hug her lightly and step back. "I'm glad. Cade loves you and he's a good person." She nodded toward the door and the full church beyond. "He has a lot of relatives here. His father is here and his mother, but I don't think they've spoken. Dirkson has another wife here, I see."

"That's Blake's mother." Blake's wife, Sierra, was her matron of honor and Sierra's mother was there, too, holding their new baby. Emily Callahan would be just two months old next week. "When Blake's daughter gets a little older, I think she'll be able to play with Amelia."

"She will." Her mother nodded. "His wife looks lovely. All the attendants do, but none more lovely than the bride. She is gorgeous."

Erin smiled again. "Thanks, Mom. The bride is the happiest person here. I can't stop smiling."

"No one wants you to. I'm sure that Cade doesn't. I don't think he can stop smiling, either."

The wedding planner poked her head in then, motioning to Erin. Her mother picked up Amelia and walked on ahead into the church. With one more glance at herself, Erin stepped out to meet her dad, who waited in the vestibule. She wrapped her arm around his and brushed a kiss on his cheek. "I love you, Daddy," she whispered, and he smiled, patting her hand.

"I love you, too. I hope you and Cade are always this happy."

"Thanks, Dad. I hope so, too." She turned from her father and looked up the aisle at Cade. The sight of him had her tingling with happiness. Her tall rancher fiancé was breathtakingly handsome in his black tux. Beside him stood Blake, the best man, and her brother and Gabe Callahan who were the groomsmen along with three of Cade's friends.

As organ music filled the church and trumpets played, the guests stood and she walked with her father until they reached the altar where her hand was placed in Cade's. She gazed into his dark blue eyes and saw the love and joy she felt reflected there.

They said their vows and Erin knew they were more than words. They were promises that she and Cade would hold forever. Then they were presented to the guests as Mr. and Mrs. Cade Callahan and as everyone applauded, they rushed back to the back of the church. After pictures, when they were in the limo on the way to the country club, Cade kissed her.

"This marriage will be good, Mrs. Callahan."

"It'll be very good," she answered, smiling at him. "Cade, I'm the happiest person on earth right now."

He shook his head. "Absolutely not. That would be

me. It's going to be great, darlin'. I promise I'm going
to do everything in my power to be the best husband
and daddy possible for you and all our kids."

She smiled at him, taking his optimistic outlook and knowing they would have kids, biological
or adopted. Either way, they would have a family
and they would be loved. She kissed him again, then
leaned back to look at him.

"Do you have a handkerchief? Wipe your mouth
where I kissed you before we get to the reception."

He grinned at her wickedly. "I'd like to just keep
going and start our honeymoon now."

"Not yet. Everyone came to party and celebrate
with us."

"It is a celebration, Erin," he said, suddenly looking serious. "A celebration that I feel can go on for
the next sixty or seventy years. We're going to have
a good marriage."

She smiled up at him. "Yes, we are," she answered,
feeling they could deal with the problems that would
come up because their love was strong.

An hour later, Cade took her hand to walk to the
dance floor at the country club for the first dance as
husband and wife. "I'm glad this first one's just for
me," he told her. "From here on out you'll have to
dance with my brothers and with yours and with as-
sorted relatives."

"My next dance is reserved for my dad."

"Well, you won't have to dance with mine. He
doesn't dance." Cade searched the crowd for his fa-

ther and found him sitting at his table. "Look at him. I don't think he's paid any attention to either of his little granddaughters, but frankly, I'm not surprised. I don't think he knows how to deal with kids, much less little girls."

Erin turned his face to her and changed the subject. "So now your brother Gabe is the only single guy in the Callahan clan. I have three friends out there who are drooling over him."

"Well, he'll like that. It won't take him long to find them if he hasn't already. Gabe likes the ladies and always has."

"I think that runs in your family," she remarked, and he grinned.

"Erin, you look so beautiful today. I will never forget watching you come down the aisle," he said.

"Thank you," she answered. Her heart beat with love for him. "I'll be glad when we're alone and I'm in your arms. We've had a lot of parties and public moments lately but now I'm ready for some private ones. And you, my very handsome husband, make my heart race to look at you. I love you, Cade Callahan. I'll spend my life showing you."

"I hope so," he said as they danced. She lost all awareness of everyone else, gazing into Cade's eyes. "Cade, I'm willing to try soon for our baby if you are."

"Darlin', I want whatever you want," he answered. "You have no idea how much I love you, but I intend to show you."

His arm tightened slightly around her waist and he drew her closer as he swept her into the dance. She couldn't imagine she could ever be happier than at that moment in his arms.

The next dance was with her father and Cade danced with his mother.

To her surprise, Dirkson Callahan asked her for the next dance. She politely danced with Cade's father. "Welcome to the Callahan clan," he said. "You're a beautiful young woman and Cade is a lucky fellow. I hear you aim to finish your education and get that PhD, which I think is commendable. I'm proud of my sons and now all of them except Gabe have married beautiful and smart women."

"Thank you. Come visit anytime. We'll be happy to have you. You can get to know your granddaughter."

"I'm not very good with children."

"She's sweet and doesn't require you to do much except smile at her. I'll show you sometime," Erin said. "Your son is a good dad."

"I'm glad to hear that because he can make up for my shortcomings." He shook his head. "But enough of family problems." He smiled at her. "Have a grand honeymoon. I told Cade I left your wedding present on his desk at his house and I have a plane to catch before too long."

"Thank you. I'm glad you were here for the wedding," she said, wondering whether he had danced with Sierra or talked much to Blake. She knew they had talked last night at the rehearsal dinner. She had seen Dirkson and all his sons standing in a circle once, talking and laughing, which surprised her after all she had heard about Blake and his feelings for his father.

Their dance ended and she turned to see Luke waiting to dance with her.

"You look beautiful, Erin," he said. "I'm glad you're happy."

"Thank you. You look quite nice yourself."

"I'm glad I told him to hire you. I've told you that before, but I'll say it again today—one last time. He'll be good for you and good to you. Cade is a good guy."

She grinned at him. "You are, too, except you're a little bossy as a big brother."

"Don't start in with me about slugging him. I've apologized sufficiently for that. How was I to know that he asked you to marry him?"

"You might have asked before you started swinging. Anyway, that's past." She patted his shoulder and looked around the room. "Isn't Amelia the prettiest little toddler?"

Luke turned to look at the child. "That she is. But I'm going to laugh when she's a teen and Cade has to deal with her."

"Cade will manage."

"Yeah, he probably will. I'm happy for both of you. I think I see his little brother lining up and focused on us. Gabe probably intends to ask you to dance next." He let out a laugh. "Besides the bride, he will dance with every beautiful single woman here. You can bet on that one and he's as opposed to marriage as Cade seemed to be, but for a different reason. Gabe just isn't ready to settle down. Cade wasn't, either, until he met you."

"I think Amelia gets the most credit for Cade wanting to settle down."

"Well, however it worked out, it's all for the best. Happy marriage, Erin," Luke said, planting a kiss on her cheek. "If you ever need me, you know you can call."

"Thanks, Luke," she said. "Thanks for coming from the South Pole for our wedding."

The music changed tempo and for the next dance most of the guests spilled out onto the floor, waving their arms and stepping in time to a lively beat while Gabe danced facing her with a big smile. When the music stopped, he placed his hand on her shoulder. "Welcome to the Callahan clan. We need you in this family, Erin. You're great for Cade and Amelia."

"Thank you. I'm happy to join the Callahan clan. And now you're related to the Dorseys, too."

"I didn't think the sun would rise on a day when I'd be related to Luke, but that's good. Luke will come back to Texas with all sorts of knowledge of penguins and icebergs and other useful stuff."

She laughed as Cade stepped to her side. "I'm claiming my bride, bro. I'm sure you can find some gorgeous single guest to flirt with."

"That's a good idea and I'm going to try my best," Gabe said, laughing and walking away.

"I'll bet I'll have white hair when he falls in love."

"You didn't think you ever would and look at you now," she said, looking at his thick black hair and wanting to run her fingers through it.

"That's because I met you," he said, gazing at her with desire in his eyes. "By the way, Dad left us a wedding present." He placed an envelope in her hand. She saw it had been opened and she saw a check inside. She looked up at Cade. He took it from her and tucked it into his pocket. "It'll go into the trust we'll set up. It's one million dollars."

"Oh, my heavens."

"That's my dad. He's all about money. Sometimes just to have him come home for Christmas would have been a bigger deal."

"I think you're already a great dad for Amelia."

He smiled at her. "Thanks. I'm trying. Let's go."

Though she was tempted to leave now with her handsome husband, she put a hand on his arm. "Soon. Just be patient and keep mingling."

They were swarmed with well-wishers and it was midafternoon when she was alone again with Cade.

"Hi. Remember me?" he asked when he sidled up to her.

She laughed. "Can we go now? I feel as if I've talked to everyone who lives in Texas."

"There are still a lot of guests here partying. Enough that I don't think we'll be missed. There's a big white limo parked and waiting in the front, and they all expect us to leave in that." He wagged his brows. "But I have a small sports car out there behind the bushes and it's ready to go. What do you say?

"I say yes to that sports car." Her parents had taken Amelia home to the ranch for a nap, and they would be babysitting her while she and Cade were on their honeymoon.

Cade didn't hesitate. "C'mon, Mrs. Callahan."

In minutes Cade drove sedately away from the church, reached the highway and sped up. Laughing, she took off her veil. "This is so much better. Now what's this surprise you have in store for me for our honeymoon?"

"Patience, love. I'll show you soon," he replied, and she laughed, her dimple showing.

Six hours later Erin stood in a sprawling one-story house of glass and stone, overlooking the blue Pacific Ocean near Monterey, California. "Cade, this is the most beautiful house and place on earth. Sure you want to stay a rancher? We can bring Amelia out here to live forever."

"I'm glad you like it. It's leased for the next six months so we can come back anytime we want. I've also leased a house in Colorado for the summer when it gets really hot at home. If you like Colorado, we can build out there and go every summer."

She threw her arms around his neck and leaned against him. For the flight she had changed to a red linen dress that ended at her knees and matching high-heeled pumps with a short matching red linen jacket. She had tossed aside the jacket.

"We'll come here or go to Colorado whenever you want—within reason," he added. "I'm adding that because I'm not leaving Texas for long periods of time."

"Oh, you're not?" she purred, rubbing her hips against him.

He shook his head. "I have plans for us there." He wrapped his arm tightly around her and kissed her passionately. She melted against him, holding him and kissing him in return, enveloped in happiness and joy. She thought of Amelia waiting at home in Texas for them and the family they had made and would add to. They'd already decided to try to have a baby as soon as possible.

Erin couldn't be happier. She was thrilled and so totally in love with her handsome Texas rancher— the man who would always make her feel loved and be a wonderful husband and a wonderful daddy for all their children.

* * * * *

#2497 THE HEIR'S UNEXPECTED BABY

Billionaires and Babies • by Jules Bennett

A billionaire investigator and his assistant vow to bring down a crime family even as they protect an orphaned baby from the fallout—and give in to their undeniable attraction! But the secrets she's keeping may destroy all they've been working for...

#2498 TWO-WEEK TEXAS SEDUCTION

Texas Cattleman's Club: Blackmail • by Cat Schield

If Brandee doesn't seduce wealthy cowboy Shane into relinquishing his claim to her ranch, she will lose everything. So she makes a wager with him—winner take all. But victory in this game of temptation may mean losing her heart...

#2499 FROM ENEMIES TO EXPECTING

Love and Lipstick • by Kat Cantrell

Billionaire Logan needs media coverage. Marketing executive Trinity needs PR buzz. And when these opposites are caught in a lip lock, *everyone* pays attention! But this fake relationship is about to turn very real when Trinity finds out she's pregnant...

#2500 ONE NIGHT WITH THE TEXAN

The Masters of Texas • by Lauren Canan

One wild, crazy night in New Orleans will change their lives forever. He doesn't want a family. She doesn't need his accusations of entrapment. Once back in Texas, will they learn the hard way that they need each other?

#2501 THE PREGNANCY AFFAIR

Accidental Heirs • by Elizabeth Bevarly

When mafia billionaire Tate Hawthorne's dark past leads him to time in a safe house, he's confined with his sexy, secret-keeping attorney Renata Twigg. Resist her for an entire week? Impossible. But this affair may have consequences...

#2502 REINING IN THE BILLIONAIRE

by Dani Wade

Once he was only the stable hand and she broke his heart. Now he's back after earning a fortune, and he vows to make her pay. But there is more to this high-society princess—and he plans to uncover it all!

REQUEST YOUR FREE BOOKS!
2 FREE NOVELS PLUS 2 FREE GIFTS!

HARLEQUIN®

Desire

ALWAYS POWERFUL, PASSIONATE AND PROVOCATIVE

YES! Please send me 2 FREE Harlequin® Desire novels and my 2 FREE gifts (gifts are worth about $10). After receiving them, if I don't wish to receive any more books, I can return the shipping statement marked "cancel." If I don't cancel, I will receive 6 brand-new novels every month and be billed just $4.55 per book in the U.S. or $5.24 per book in Canada. That's a savings of at least 13% off the cover price! It's quite a bargain! Shipping and handling is just 50¢ per book in the U.S. and 75¢ per book in Canada.* I understand that accepting the 2 free books and gifts places me under no obligation to buy anything. I can always return a shipment and cancel at any time. Even if I never buy another book, the two free books and gifts are mine to keep forever.

225/326 HDN GH2P

Name	(PLEASE PRINT)

Address	Apt. #

City	State/Prov.	Zip/Postal Code

Signature (if under 18, a parent or guardian must sign)

Mail to the **Reader Service**:
IN U.S.A.: P.O. Box 1867, Buffalo, NY 14240-1867
IN CANADA: P.O. Box 609, Fort Erie, Ontario L2A 5X3

Want to try two free books from another line?
Call 1-800-873-8635 or visit www.ReaderService.com.

* Terms and prices subject to change without notice. Prices do not include applicable taxes. Sales tax applicable in N.Y. Canadian residents will be charged applicable taxes. Offer not valid in Quebec. This offer is limited to one order per household. Not valid for current subscribers to Harlequin Desire books. All orders subject to credit approval. Credit or debit balances in a customer's account(s) may be offset by any other outstanding balance owed by or to the customer. Please allow 4 to 6 weeks for delivery. Offer available while quantities last.

Your Privacy—The Reader Service is committed to protecting your privacy. Our Privacy Policy is available online at www.ReaderService.com or upon request from the Reader Service.

We make a portion of our mailing list available to reputable third parties that offer products we believe may interest you. If you prefer that we not exchange your name with third parties, or if you wish to clarify or modify your communication preferences, please visit us at www.ReaderService.com/consumerchoice or write to us at Reader Service Preference Service, P.O. Box 9062, Buffalo, NY 14240-9062. Include your complete name and address.

HD15

SPECIAL EXCERPT FROM

HARLEQUIN®

Desire

A billionaire investigator and his assistant vow to bring down a crime family even as they protect an orphaned baby from the fallout—and give in to their undeniable attraction! But the secrets she's keeping may destroy all they've been working for...

Read on for a sneak peek at
THE HEIR'S UNEXPECTED BABY
by Jules Bennett, part of the bestselling
BILLIONAIRES AND BABIES series!

"What are you doing here so early?"

Jack Carson brushed past Vivianna Smith and stepped into her apartment, trying like hell not to touch her. Or breathe in that familiar jasmine scent. Or think of how sexy she looked in that pale pink suit.

Masochist. That's all he could chalk this up to. But he had a mission, damn it, and he needed his assistant's help to pull it off.

"I need you to use that charm of yours and get more information about the O'Sheas." He turned to face her as she closed the door.

The O'Sheas might run a polished high-society auction house, but he knew they were no better than common criminals. And Jack was about to bring them down in a spectacular show of justice. His ticket was the woman who fueled his every fantasy.

Vivianna moved around him to head down the hall to the nursery. "I'm on your side here," she told him with a soft smile. "Why don't you come back this evening and I'll make dinner and we can figure out our next step."

Dinner? With her and the baby? That all sounded so… domestic. He prided himself on keeping work in the office or in neutral territory. But he'd come here this morning to check on her…and he couldn't blame it all on the O'Sheas.

Damn it.

"You can come to my place and I'll have my chef prepare something." There. If Tilly was on hand, then maybe it wouldn't seem so family-like. "Any requests?" he asked.

Did her gaze just dart to his lips? She couldn't look at him with those dark eyes as if she wanted…

No. It didn't matter what she wanted, or what he wanted for that matter. Their relationship was business only.

Jack paused, soaking in the sight of her in that prim little suit, holding the baby. Definitely time to go before he forgot she actually worked for him and took what he'd wanted for months…

Don't miss
THE HEIR'S UNEXPECTED BABY
by Jules Bennett,
available February 2017 wherever
Harlequin® Desire books and ebooks are sold.

If you enjoyed this excerpt, pick up a new
BILLIONAIRES AND BABIES *book every month!*

It's the #1 bestselling series from Harlequin® Desire—
Powerful men…wrapped around their babies' little
fingers.

www.Harlequin.com

Whatever You're Into… Passionate Reads

Looking for more passionate reads from Harlequin®?
Fear not! Harlequin® Presents, Harlequin® Desire and
Harlequin® Blaze offer you irresistible romance stories
featuring powerful heroes.

❋HARLEQUIN *Presents.*

Do you want alpha males, decadent glamour and jet-set
lifestyles? Step into the sensational, sophisticated world of
Harlequin® Presents, where sinfully tempting heroes ignite a
fierce and wickedly irresistible passion!

❋HARLEQUIN *Desire*

Harlequin® Desire novels are powerful, passionate and
provocative contemporary romances set against a backdrop of
wealth, privilege and sweeping family saga. Alpha heroes with
a soft side meet strong-willed but vulnerable heroines amid a
dramatic world of divided loyalties, high-stakes conflict and
intense emotion.

❋HARLEQUIN *Blaze*

Harlequin® Blaze stories sizzle with strong heroines and
irresistible heroes playing the game of modern love and lust.
They're fun, sexy and always steamy.

Be sure to check out our full selection of books
within each series every month!

www.Harlequin.com

HPASSION2016

Turn your love of reading into rewards you'll love with

Harlequin My Rewards

Join for FREE today at www.HarlequinMyRewards.com

Earn **FREE BOOKS** of your choice.

Experience **EXCLUSIVE OFFERS** and contests.

Enjoy **BOOK RECOMMENDATIONS** selected just for you.

PLUS! Sign up now and get **500** points right away!

Earn
FREE
REWARDS
HarlequinMyRewards.com
Join
Today!

MYR16R